Why Should I Love You? 2

Ivy Symone

Acknowledgments

Thank you....

Prologue

12 Years Ago...

Fifteen-year-old Lovely felt an imminent threat to her life as it dangled over her like a dark cloud. It was evident in the faces of her parents Dharmesh and Naomi.

Lovely's father, a South Indian native, Dharmesh Prasad was a hard-working amiable man. His money was long, and he took pride in providing his family's every need and want. The Prasads were in the business of resorts and casinos all over the world. Dharmesh ventured out on his own in the convenience store business. He was a very humble, earnest, and forthright man. He was loved and adored by many. His number one fan was his only child, Lovely. His second biggest fan was a toss-up between his mother and his wife Naomi, a beautiful African American model. Dharmesh was crazy about his wife and daughter. He would go to the ends of the world and back for them.

But, something was going down. Lovely stood back out of the way watching as her father spoke with her mother, Naomi. They were arguing. Not yelling arguing; however, it was something deep. Naomi's facial expression told Lovely her mother was mad and scared.

Dharmesh walked away. Naomi said to his back, "Lovely and I are leaving in the morning."

He stopped and looked back at her. "No, you're not. I will protect you like I'm supposed to." He said with earnest sincerity.

Naomi fought back the tears. "I don't feel safe."

"But you are." He said, feeling pressed for time as he gazed down at his expensive Cartier watch. "I will be back before supper. I love you."

Naomi was so displeased she didn't reciprocate the words. Dharmesh understood. He proceeded to join his security team that was waiting for him.

Naomi turned around and saw Lovely standing where the hallway opened to the foyer. Naomi smiled weakly. "Hey, Love."

"Is everything okay, Mama?" Lovely asked.

Naomi seemed to float as her long summer dress grazed the marble floor. She placed her arm around Lovely's shoulder. "Baby, everything is just fine. Now, wouldn't it be nice to go pay Aunt Livy and all of our cousins a visit?"

"Yes," Lovely replied, but she wasn't dumb. Her mother wasn't fond of her family. Any time Naomi was willing to take a trip to go visit them, something was definitely wrong.

———

Dharmesh made it back home, but it was much later than the time he stated. No sooner than he could get in the door, a cold blow was shot to the back of his head. He was knocked unconscious, and then dragged across the sleek marble floor into the family room.

Lovely was already asleep while the invasion was taking place. Her dreams came to a sudden end as she felt her body move out of the comfortable position she had been laying. It wasn't that her body was just moved; it was snatched. Jolting out of her sleep she immediately sensed something was wrong. Her reaction was to scream. Hands grabbed her. A hand covered her mouth and nose. After a couple of seconds, there was total blackness, and as she awakened, something hard and cold greeted her head, and a voice snarled.

"Don't say a fuckin word or I'll shoot your mothafuckin brains out."

She was blindfolded and bound at the arms and legs. The invaders spoke amongst themselves in Spanish. Her father begged. "Please don't hurt my daughter!"

Lovely could hear her mother sobbing as if she already knew their fate. Lovely began to cry out to her father.

"Shut the fuck up! All of you," someone spat angrily. "What's the code to the mothafuckin vault?"

There was silence. Then Lovely heard a cracking sound as the body of a gun connected with Dharmesh's head. Naomi screamed out.

The people invading their home started taunting and torturing Naomi and Lovely. When Lovely no longer heard her father, she assumed he was unconscious. Naomi was stubborn and refused to make things easy.

"Get the fuck out of our house! Leave my family alone!" She yelled out, causing added fuel to an already blazing flame.

The invaders spoke in Spanish again. Next thing Lovely knew, she was being snatched up again and dragged out of the room. Lovely cried and wanted to fight, but the duct tape gave

9

very little room for her to move. She knew what was about to happen. To get Naomi to cooperate, they began to torture her sexually with very brutal force."

"She's pretty," one of the invaders said. "I see why her husband is so protective."

Begging them not to, Naomi still wouldn't provide the code. She was the hardest woman to break as the men continued to torture her any kind of way they could think of. It wasn't until Lovely began screaming out loud as she was being sexually abused by one of the guys, that Dharmesh regained consciousness. Immediately hearing what was happening, Dharmesh surrendered. "Stop! Let my daughter go. Please do not hurt her! I will give you the code."

It was too late for fifteen-year-old Lovely as she lay there helpless. One of the ruthless invaders had already invaded the most precious thing in the world to her, to every girl, even to her parents, her virginity.

Another presence showed up before the next guy could have his way. "Get to the got damn vault!" The newcomer ordered. "Stop all of this other bullshit. *Y date prisa!*"

Lovely's blindfold had moved out of place. The guy running his mouth didn't realize that his sleeve had come up above his wrist, showing off his demonic creature tattoo. She could clearly see it on his yellow skin tone. That was something that she vowed in her mind that she'd never forget as she gazed at it, still in shock that all of this was taking place. The guy noticed that she could somewhat see him as he leaned down closer to her. The scowl on his face reminded her that she wasn't supposed to see him. She looked away quickly, but it was too late.

"Why this bitch's blindfold off?" he barked as he struck her across the face. "Don't fucking look at me!"

Lovely felt like her head would snap off. She cried softly not wanting to upset the invaders. She kept her head lowered.

"*Este estúpido coño hizo,*" another one of the invaders said in reference to the one that raped their young captive.

Once the vault had been emptied of all of its contents, the invaders put a bullet in Naomi's head and then one in Dharmesh. Lovely let out a blood-curdling cry. She knew that she was about to die, and she may as well accept it. Lovely's spirit was so violated she didn't even react when the gun pressed up to her head. There was hesitance. The newcomer ordered that they go ahead and set fire to the house. Lovely thought for a brief second, they would let her live.

The newcomer said, "Kill that bitch too." Before walking away, one of the men shot her in the back of the head. Everything went black.

Chapter One

Present Day...

Lovely had just told Abe that she was pregnant and was waiting for a response. She wasn't sure if this was the exact reaction she was expecting, but the silence that met her ears was a bit awkward. *Okay*, she thought. *Why isn't he saying anything?*

"Abe?" Lovely questioned softly.

Abe could only blink at the news Lovely just revealed. There was definitely an excitement there that Abe felt deep within. However, it could not break through the befuddled state he was currently in after realizing that he was the man responsible for her condition. The disappointment within him mixed with anger clearly showed on his face. It was moments like this that he was glad she couldn't make out the details of his expression.

Eli asked with concern, "You alright Abe? Lovely just told you she's pregnant. Isn't that great news? She's about to be carrying your big-headed ass baby."

Considering the distressed state Abe was in just moments before, David was unsure if he should even crack a smile at Eli's attempt to lighten the mood. The look Abe gave Eli was enough to guarantee David's silence for the moment.

"Say something," Eli pressed.

Ike cleared his throat as he took a step towards the door, but not before giving Abe a slighted look. "C'mon Eli. Perhaps we should give them some privacy."

When Eli didn't budge, Ike grabbed him by the arm to pull him along. "Will you come on?"

Lovely looked towards Eli, Ike, and David and said, "We'll be just a second."

Once the door closed behind them, the silence returned. Lovely turned her attention back to Abe. "Baby, what's wrong?"

Unable to look at Lovely, Abe focused on the mark that was left on his truck after he threw the bucket.

Lovely shifted her weight to lean away from his body. Her hands fell away from his head as she looked down upon him. She wished she could make out the details of his face to read him. She was not liking the vibe she was getting from him. His body language was closed off as if he didn't want to let her in on how he was really feeling. There was a silent barrier between them.

Wanting to end the awkward silence, Lovely decided to veer in another direction. "I'm sorry I didn't get back in time to meet your friend Eric," she said apologetically.

Finally, he spoke, "He had to leave."

"I know. So, did you enjoy his visit?" she asked cheerfully. She hoped to lighten the mood. The atmosphere was dismal and Lovely didn't like it. The vibe between them had always been upbeat and jubilant.

"It was okay," Abe said somberly.

There was silence again.

Lovely began to sense the worst. Was Abe ready to call it quits? It had only been a few months, but it felt like years of being in love with him. What Lovely loved the most about Abe was that he truly loved her. It wasn't about just hearing him say the words, "I love you"; she got that all of the time. It was his actions. Everything he did for her, to her, about her, with her was laced with pure love. Another reason Lovely adored her man so much was because he knew hurt, pain and raw emotion. He was very sensitive, always looking for love. Lovely had assured him time and time again he didn't need to look any further because she had all of the love he ever would need.

Lovely asked with concern, "Are you okay?"

His head lowered. Nothing came from his mouth.

"Abe?" Lovely moved back into his space. Afraid that he would recoil from her touch, Lovely carefully reached out and rubbed his back. "You can talk to me."

"It's nothing," he mumbled.

"It gotta be something," Lovely countered. "I mean, I told you I was pregnant, and you hadn't even say anything about it."

"I just got a lot weighing heavily on my mind," he tried to explain.

Lovely responded quickly with, "Well how do you feel about us having a baby?"

Again, no response.

Lovely shook her head in disbelief. She let her hand fall from his back. "I thought the two of us having a baby is something you want."

"It was what I wanted."

"Was?"

"I mean...it is," he said with uncertainty. He looked at Lovely and in an accusatory tone asked, "How are you pregnant anyway, and you just had a period?"

His tone was offensive; Lovely was taken aback as she explained carefully, "I'm irregular. You know that. I guess I have periods when I'm pregnant because I did the same with Grace."

"But how do you know you're pregnant? You've already been to a doctor?"

"Not my obstetrician. I went to my family doctor because I was feeling really tired and having these light-headed spells," Lovely said. She went on. "Aunt Livy told me I needed to go get checked out. When she said I was pregnant, I was like you. How could I be? Aunt Livy had to remind me about my pregnancy with Grace. I thought I just needed a B12 shot or something."

"So why didn't you tell me about this?" Abe asked. Again, his tone was somewhat harsh.

"Well...I'm telling you now," Lovely said with hesitance. She could sense an edge in Abe's tone. He let out a heavy sigh that put Lovely in a state of uneasiness. Lovely frowned. Was a baby what Abe really wanted? He stayed so busy. When would he have time to even play Daddy? When Abe was home, he was always working in the office or sketching or putting digital designs together or working on a model. He had business trips that lasted two days at a time. He was still actively involved in GVBC and TAV. Was he ready for a baby? Was she really ready for another baby?

Abe abruptly got up from the bench brushing past her in the process. He headed to the door leading into the house.

"Abe?" Lovely called.

He stopped before reaching the door. "What Lovely?"

"What's the matter? Have this between us already gotten boring to you?"

He didn't say anything. Lovely walked over to him. Her soft and cautious tenor began to fade. Abe sensed the sudden change in her attitude.

She asked, "Are you seeing someone else? Is it Aisha? Is she really pregnant by you and you don't know how to tell me? If that's it I've already gotten myself used to the idea. It's not a deal breaker for me because you were with her before me."

"No Lovely," he said in an aggravated tone. "That's not it."

"So, there is an issue. If it's not Aisha, then maybe it's another woman. Tell me, Abe."

"There is nothing to tell. I'm not seeing another woman. Don't want to."

"Then why are you treating me so different? I don't understand. And I told you I was pregnant, and you act like you could care less."

Abe couldn't reply.

Lovely sighed heavily with perplexity. "You know what Abe. I can't do this with you. I'm not used to this, and I have really low tolerance for nonsense and bullshit. This right here seems like some bullshit. I told you from the get-go that—"

"So, what are you saying Lovely? Because I can't confirm for you that I'm seeing another woman, which I'm not, you wanna throw the towel in based off your assumption?" Abe asked angrily.

"If you can't answer me or even talk to me about what's going on with you...Like I said. My tolerance is low. You can leave."

"What the fuck?" he said in disbelief. "Are you serious? For a woman who claims she love me; it could be that easy to get rid of me. Just like that?"

"What did I say? I'm not into sharing or being second options." Lovely remained firm. She crossed her arms over her breasts.

"Whatever Lovely," he murmured opening the door to enter the house.

"Yeah, well maybe she can comfort you, and you'll talk to her!" she yelled after him still standing in the garage.

Lovely waited on a response she knew she wouldn't get. The worst part about it was she already craved for his presence. What just happened? She asked herself.

The life Lovely had with her man was everything a woman could dream of. Abe was perfect in every way imaginable. She loved his big strong arms that held her at night until the morning came. The soothing sounds of his voice that caressed the inside of her ears. The soft kisses he left behind starting from the top of her head to the tips of her toes. His laughter. His emotions. His thoughtfulness and loving, sensitive ways. She found her a winner in Abe.

It didn't matter that he was wealthy, but she admired that he was successful. His material things were irrelevant to her. What mattered to her was the testimony of his hard work and determination. His looks were the least of Lovely's concern for it was not his looks that attracted her to him in the first place. Lovely was unable to see the details of the pretty face other people had the privilege of adoring. However, Lovely appreciated what his personality had to offer.

With all that being considered Lovely felt it was the appropriate time to tell Abe about the pregnancy. She didn't expect him to react the way he did though. The pregnancy had come as a shock to her as well, but she felt that the news would have overjoyed him. It was what they had discussed many times. And now there was indifference coming from Abe. Lovely didn't get it.

———

Abe drove with no particular destination in mind. He just needed to gather his thoughts and become accepting of the news he had received. It was hard. He was trying to accept this as reality. This was the most fucked up feeling he have had in years.

"Fuck!" Abe groaned. He took his frustration out on his stirring wheel by hitting it several times. He asked himself aloud, "What am I gonna do? What the fuck am I gonna do?"

At that moment, a call came through. It was Kenya, his ex. *What do she want,* he wondered? He pressed the answer button on his steering wheel to accept the call. "Hello?"

"Hey, stranger!" Kenya said excitedly.

"Hey," Abe responded dryly.

"Am I catching you at a bad time?" she asked.

"No. What's up?"

"I was just calling to see what you've been up to. I hadn't heard from you much since I've been back."

"Yeah, I know. I've been busy," he said. He started to grow impatient with the conversation. "Kenya, can I call you back?"

"Well I guess so," she said with hesitance. She asked quickly, "Are you okay? You don't sound that great."

Abe sighed heavily, "I'm just going through a lil something at the moment."

"Do you wanna talk about it?"

"Not really."

"I hate to hear you so sad. How about I meet you somewhere and help you take your mind off things for a little while?" she suggested.

"I don't know if it will really help this," he said hopelessly.

"Let me be your friend. I mean I know you better than anybody. We can go grab a drink or something and talk about old times."

Would that really help? Abe wondered. It would give him something to do. He couldn't keep riding around with nowhere to go because it definitely wasn't helping any.

———

Agreeing to meet Kenya for a drink at Bella's had proven to be a good idea at first. Talking about the past and the good times they had shared had put Abe's mind at ease momentarily. However, Abe wasn't so sure that following Kenya back to her home was a smart choice.

"What's wrong Abe?" Kenya asked softly. They were in her living room and sitting on the sofa next to one another. Things had taken a turn in the wrong direction for Abe; however, it was everything right for Kenya.

19

Abe looked at Kenya's lips. They were as soft as he remembered. The kiss they had just shared proved that. The kiss also brought him back to his reality. Being with Kenya had offered Abe a distraction from his current dilemma with Lovely. He didn't want to think about Lovely at that moment. He wanted to push that problem far back in the corner of his mind and leave it there.

Abe shook his head. He stood to his feet saying, "I think I need to get going."

"You know you're welcomed to stay here," she said. She hopped up from her sofa ready to stop him.

"I can't," Abe told her.

"Is it because of the blind girl?" Kenya asked forwardly.

Thoughts of Lovely resurfaced. He could see her bright and warm smile. He was so in love with Lovely. So why was he here kissing on his ex-girlfriend? Had he not hurt Lovely enough? He didn't need to add on to the damage he already done although it was unknown to Lovely. Being with Kenya and ending up in a compromising situation was the last thing he needed to do.

When Abe didn't respond, Kenya said, "I thought maybe you two were going to stop seeing each other."

Abe's brow furrowed with confusion. He asked, "Why would you think that?"

Kenya said, "Kiera told me that some stuff was probably about to go down between you and that girl."

Now Abe was curious to know what else Kiera had informed Kenya. "What did she mean by that?"

Feeling as if she had said too much, Kenya waved her hands in the air as if to dismiss it all, "Look, I'm just going to leave it alone. You ask Kiera what she meant by that."

Growing agitated, Abe snapped, "No, you tell me what the fuck she told you!"

Kenya sat back down on her sofa. "I don't know anything."

"Tell me what she said Kenya," Abe demanded sternly.

Flippantly, Kenya replied, "Something about you, Ghost and Loco killing her father."

Abe could feel himself boiling inside. Why was Kiera running her fucking mouth!

Abe abruptly turned and went to the door. Kenya said to him, "Abe, I'm here for you. You know when that girl finds out, it's not going to be—"

Abe cut her off by walking out and slamming the door behind him.

———

Abe found himself driving to his brother's house to sort out his thoughts.

Confusion had clouded Abe's thinking. Love had caused him to be in such a state. He loved Lovely with every fiber of his being, but he knew he didn't deserve her. He didn't have a right to love her, and she love him in return. Not after what he had done. How could he be with her now?

As he laid in bed thoughts of the past and present swirled in his head. It was so easy to forget and get facts mixed up. Abe had done so much wrongdoing he had learn to disassociate himself from it. Whenever he did anything, he remained disconnected. He had conditioned himself to forget some of the horrible things he had done to people. It wasn't him anymore. If he forgot the past, it was almost as if he hadn't done them. Extreme case of denial.

Antino Mancuso, a very urbane and polished Italian guy who was running a large organized crime operation out of Boston, had relocated to the quieter and slower paced city of Nashville following in the footsteps of one of his allies. It was then that Antino ran into a troubled teenager looking to release the hell within him. Antino had taken Abe in when he was a teenager and showed him the world of wrongdoings. Antino showed him a love that Abe lacked at home so doing whatever Antino asked was like showing Abe's gratitude and appreciation.

Antino helped mold Abe into Fyah, his alter ego. Abe was his favorite and got a lot of hate thrown his way for it too. Antino called on Abe and begged him to do one last job that would pay him so good he wouldn't have to ever worry about money again. Unable to resist Abe agreed to the job. At the time Abe was about 75% finished with the street life, but he would do an occasional bid here and there if it meant a large sum of money. Abe was in school and was concentrating on moving on to doing legit things like his company he was investing so much of his money in.

Abe's phone started ringing again. It was Lovely. He still needed time to face Lovely without the guilt.

Abe pondered the thought of his current situation in his head over and over. No matter which way he thought of his existing dilemma he couldn't come up with any answers. His mind drew a blank. It was too much for his mind to wrap around. The best thing at the moment was to let sleep take over.

Chapter Two

*A*re you still coming?

As Robin walked up to him, Eli responded to the text: *Give me 30*

"Were you staying here with me?" Robin asked eyeing the cellphone in Eli's hand.

Eli looked up from his phone and said, "No, I'm going home tonight."

"Well I can come over there then," Robin said.

"Uhm...no," Eli said carefully. "I sorta kinda wanna..."

Robin nodded with understanding although she showed disappointment. "I get it. You have other plans."

"Well, it's not that," Eli was saying as he became aware of the apparent lie he was about to tell. Why did he feel a need to lie? Robin wasn't his woman; however, he felt a need to coddle her feelings.

Robin smiled sweetly. "I understand Eli. It's okay. I'll just hang out with you another time."

Eyeing the fiery orange of her hair to the smooth softness of her milky beige skin, Eli was tempted to dismiss his prior plans. Being with Robin felt like being with a real woman. It felt good. The sex was fulfilling. Falling asleep while holding her was comforting. It was something Eli felt he could get used to. However, he wasn't sure if he was ready to give up his singlehood to commit to Robin on a full-time basis.

Eli's phone chimed notifying him of a text received. It was from Kris again. *The door is unlocked. Let yourself in.*

Right, he thought. He had to get to Kris. He didn't have time to get lost in thoughts of Robin. He looked down at Robin, "I'll call you later."

Robin nodded in acknowledgment.

Eli went on to walk away, but Robin caught him by the arm. "Can I get a kiss or a hug or something?"

Hell no, Eli thought.

Kiera walked by turning her nose up at the two of them. "Kiss and a hug?"

Robin rolled her eyes in annoyance. "You know what? Never mind Eli. I'll just talk with you later." She walked away but not before cutting her eyes at Kiera.

Kiera let out a hearty laugh as she continued into the kitchen. Eli shook his head at Kiera, but he was grateful for her interruption.

"Why you ain't give your girlfriend a kiss and hug?" Kiera teased.

Eli walked over to the breakfast bar. "She's not my girlfriend."

Kiera made a noise signifying her skepticism. "Really? Coulda fooled me."

"That's because you're easily fooled," Eli retorted. His eyes trailed down to the curves of her ass. Kiera was indeed a very fine woman, but she was too devious for Eli's taste. He asked, "When are we going to take the DNA tests Kee?"

Kiera rolled her eyes in exasperation. "Eli, please. Not this again."

"Yes, this again. Look, if I'm not their father I want to see it in black and white," Eli said seriously.

Kiera mocked him as she helped herself to a piece of the cake Aunt Livy had made.

Eli detested Kiera's unwillingness to cooperate on the paternity of her twins, Bria and Bryce. If the twins were his children, Eli definitely wanted to step up to the plate and be their father. It was a shame they were eight years of age, and he was just getting to know them.

"I'll see about it. Okay, Eli?" Kiera said with an attitude.

"Don't say that shit just to appease me," Eli warned.

Kiera fed her face with a chunk of cake. With her mouth full she murmured, "I'm not...We'll get it done."

"Didn't sound really convincing," Eli said. "But I'ma stay on your ass about this."

Kiera smirked up at him with a hint of seduction. "You sure you don't wanna be *up in* this ass instead?"

Eli responded by walking away. *There she go*, he thought. He chuckled inwardly at himself. The thought of fucking Kiera was tantalizing though.

————

Kris could hardly contain her excitement. She was overjoyed that Eli had showed up considering how he had been treating her lately. Although she wanted to enjoy a drama free night with him, she wanted to make him aware of how she felt of his recent mistreatment to her. He made her hide because of another woman? Really?

"Kris?" Eli called as he made his way down the hallway to her bedroom.

She remained quiet but kept her eyes on the doorway of her bedroom. Eli walked into the darkened room.

"Why you got it so damn dark in here?" Eli asked.

When she saw him go for the light switch, Kris spoke, "Leave it off."

The only light that illuminated the room came from the glow of the thirty-two-inch television. "You know I like to see," Eli said as he made his way to her bed where she was laying.

"I know," Kris said softly.

Eli stared at Kris. Something wasn't right. Despite how dark it was in the room Eli could see there was something different about Kris. He went for the lamp on her nightstand.

"No!" Kris objected, but it was too late. His eyes immediately shifted to her head. Kris was starting to feel uncomfortable and embarrassed at the same time. Averting her eyes, she asked, "What?"

"What the hell is that on your head?" Eli asked. His face was mixed with amusement and confusion.

Kris' hands self-consciously went to the lace front wig she was wearing. "You don't like it?"

"You look like you about to participate in a samurai fight. What is that? A lace front?" he asked with his face screwed up in dislike.

"Yeah, it is. I thought I'd do something different."

"I hate lace front wigs," Eli stated matter of factly. "Why didn't you at least get the one with baby hair?"

Kris stared at him blankly. Eli returned the same stare. He leaned over to pet the wig like it was some kind of animal. Kris swatted at him. He backed away trying to stifle a laugh. Feeling slighted, Kris cut her eyes at him and focused on the television.

Eli frowned but was amused. The wig was definitely different from the low natural cut she wore. She looked completely different. "Kris?"

"What Eli?" Kris asked dryly.

"What's up with this look of yours?" Eli asked sitting down on the edge of the bed.

With her eyes glued to the television, Kris answered, "I figure you wanted a girlie girl. So here I am."

"But this isn't you."

"But it's what you like. Right?" She asked turning to face him.

"I like whatever. Have I ever complained about how you looked before?"

"You don't have to say it out loud. Your actions and how you treat me tell me enough."

"So, you think by putting on this shiny ass wig will make me treat you any different?" he asked.

"I would hope it would," Kris said with an attitude.

"The way you look ain't got nothing to do with the way things are between you and me," Eli pointed out.

"I didn't say anything about the way things were between us. I'm talking about how you treat me," she said as her voice slightly raised.

"How do I treat you?" he asked with irritation.

"Like shit," she mumbled.

"Like shit? I treat you like shit?"

"Yes!" her voice raised. The mood had definitely taken a shift.

"Who the hell you yelling at?" Eli asked angrily.

"You!" Kris yelled.

"You know what," Eli said as he got up. "Why the fuck am I here?"

Kris stared up at him feeling herself getting angry. *I know he ain't about to leave,* she thought. "Where are you going?"

"I'm leaving. I didn't come over here to have this little spat with you. I came over here to fuck, and that's it."

Kris stared at him in disbelief; shocked by his blunt honesty. "Really Eli?"

Maybe Eli didn't mean it, but at this point, Kris was getting on his nerves, and he hadn't been there five minutes. Eli's mind was on several things. One of them still being Abe and what was going on with him. Earlier Abe was acting strange, and he wasn't talking about what was bothering him. Lovely revealed that she was pregnant, and Abe ended up leaving. Whatever was weighing on Abe's mind, it was something extremely intense.

Eli ignored Kris' desperate gaze and headed to the bedroom door. Kris jumped out of bed and was right behind him.

"Eli, okay I'm sorry," Kris said with desperation. She grabbed his arm to stop him. "Don't leave. I just wanna be whatever I need to be so that you will love me back."

Eli sighed with annoyance and rolled his eyes. "Don't start that love shit, Kris. Let go of my arm so I can go."

Disobeying his order, she continued to hold onto him and asked, "Do you love her?"

"Love who?"

"Robin."

"The only person I love in this equation is me."

"So why did you do what you did last week?"

Eli didn't have an answer for her.

"You made me hide because you didn't want that bitch to know I was there. Why isn't she made aware of who I am? How come she came first, and you threw me to the side?"

"I told you what was up with that Kris. I'm not gonna keep repeating myself either."

"Okay," Kris said softly. Her voice quivered as she looked up into his eyes and asked, "So is this all we have?"

"What do you mean?"

"Between us. I mean, should I never expect more from you? Ever?"

"I don't know," Eli said. He was giving her a hard time, but even as he stood there looking down at her soft feminine features, Eli knew his feelings for Kris were more than he wanted to admit. He just wasn't ready to go there. Additionally, he wasn't sure where he wanted things to go with Robin.

Kris grabbed his hands into hers. "Don't leave just yet."

"I don't wanna argue Kris."

"I won't. I'm letting that go. Just stay here with me," she pleaded. She began to walk backward pulling him along. He offered no resistance as Kris led him to her bed. She asked, "What do you need from me tonight?"

A smile formed on Eli's lips. "You know what I need."

Kris sat down on the side of her bed pulling Eli in front of her. Keeping her gaze locked on his she began to unbuckle his belt. "I'll take care of your every need."

———

Two can play that game, Robin thought. Who did Eli think he was hurting? Certainly not her. Robin had options just like he had options. The only difference was that hers came with a wife on the side.

Robin went to the tenth-floor penthouse suite as instructed. Before she could tap on the door, it opened, and he was grinning at her. He stepped aside ushering her in. "Come on in."

Robin was impressed by the inside furnishings and décor of the suite. The wall of floor to ceiling windows to the right caught her attention. There were no window dressings obstructing the view of the nightlife below of downtown Nashville.

Awestricken, Robin, slowly made her way to the windows. "This is really nice."

"You like it?" he asked. He was now holding a small glass of amber colored liquor. He slowly made his way over to where Robin stood. "Nice view, huh?"

"The view is awesome!" Robin's eyes widen as she smiled brightly. She looked below at the bright lights coming from the LP Field. The lights reflected off the Cumberland River.

Robin turned to him still wearing an excited smile. "When did you get this place?"

He gave her a cocky smile. "Don't you worry about that. Just know that we no longer have to worry about the hotel again."

"So, what are you saying?" Robin asked sweetly.

"I'm saying," he said as he carefully wrapped his arms around her. He planted a kiss on her lips. "This is ours."

Robin gave him a doubtful look. "Ours?"

He backed away from her wearing a frown. "You don't like it? I thought you liked it."

"Oh, I do," she said returning her gaze to the view below. This was too easy, Robin thought. She just told him last week he had to do something about his wife. Now he was calling an obvious expensive condo "theirs." How convenient. The smile she once wore had faded into a look of worry.

"What's wrong with you?" he asked. Robin could hear the concern in the softness of his voice.

"Nothing," she mumbled. Her thoughts shifted to Eli. She tried to shake feelings of Eli, but he was on her mind. Who in the hell was he seeing? Robin hoped it wasn't that damn Kiera.

"You seem bothered."

I'm fine, she thought to herself. Or am I? Robin wanted more. She wanted what Lovely had with Abe. What they had was like a dream. It was perfect. They were affectionate, respectful, never argued and they were into each other. It amazed Robin to watch Abe when he looked at Lovely. Robin could see the love all in his face. He loved Lovely. So why couldn't Robin have that? She thought she could be in love with Eli and Eli be just as in love with her. But Eli wasn't free with his emotions like Abe was.

He reached over taking her hands in his. "I miss you."

Robin glanced at their intertwined hands. She let her eyes travel up until they met with his. Softly, she said, "I miss you too."

He touched her face endearingly, "You don't seem like you do. Baby, what's wrong?"

Ignoring him, Robin gazed up into his eyes and asked, "What about your divorce?"

"It will happen. Do you not trust me?"

"I want to trust that you will do what you say you will do."

"And I am," he said. He placed a kiss on her lips. He smiled down at Robin causing his eyes to twinkle. "I really did miss you. I don't even know why you cut me off in the first place. This other guy must not be what you thought he was or you wouldn't be here with me," he said. He admired the softness of her face. He loved this girl, but she was always tripping.

"It wasn't about him. I cut you off because you're married."

"But you know my situation." He said walking away and heading towards the kitchen. It was an open floor plan; therefore, Robin was able to keep her eyes on him as he moved about. He looked in her direction and asked, "Have you started fucking him?"

"That's none of your business."

"It is my business. This wasn't about you falling in love with another fucking man, Robin. You were supposed to be loving me. And you flipped on me. So, I can only assume you are fucking him." His aggravation became evident.

"Well...," she said with hesitance.

"You didn't have to fuck him," he said angrily through clenched teeth.

"Are you still fucking your wife?" Robin retorted. She made her way across the living room floor to join him in the kitchen.

Of course, he was still fucking his wife; when she was in the mood. "That bitch don't fuck. Her fucking hormones are off."

They stood there staring at each other with thoughts of their own swirling in their heads. With other issues on his mind, He disturbed the silence that had been lingering as he cleared his throat and asked, "So how is business?"

Robin smirked confidently. "It's good. The foundation has been receiving hefty donations."

"She still doesn't know?"

"Nope," she said.

With a sinister grin, he said, "I need a hundred thousand."

Robin's eyes grew big in disbelief. "Really? That much? Why such a large amount?"

"How long have you been transferring funds Robin?" he asked with sarcasm. "I'm pretty sure it's in there plus some."

"But I thought your finances were straight. Why would you need that much?"

He scoffed as he gestured with his hands showcasing the condo before her. "You think this shit came from out of thin air? This condo won't pay for itself."

"That much?"

He gave her an impatient look. "Now you know you're not in the position to play around. It'll be a shame for your friend to find out that you've been stealing from her."

Robin hated being at the mercy of anyone. She thought this was the one thing she could be in control of; however, he had proven that wrong. "When do you need it?"

"As soon as you can get it to me," he said.

"Okay," she said. She looked at the fully decorated and furnished posh condo. "Uhm E, this condo is worth more than a hundred thousand dollars."

"I know that," he said in a condescending tone. "Just get me the money and let me worry about everything else."

"So, what about us?"

He frowned. "What do you mean?"

"Will we continue to see each other?"

"I never said we would stop. You're the one that try to come up with ultimatums and run to the next nigga."

Robin lowered her head with hopelessness. Shaking her head, she said, "I don't know. It just seems as though it will never be more than what it is."

"It is baby. My wife means nothing. I just gotta play it out right. That bitch is greedy and will try to leave me with nothing."

Robin nodded gazing out not focused on anything in particular. "I just feel so…," she let her words trail off.

He softened the tone of his voice. "Look, you started something that you can't turn back on now. Put that guilt shit aside and focus Robin."

"I am."

"For right now this is how we will do things. But I have something bigger planned for your friend. This should have us set for life. I can divorce my wife, and it can be you and me living far away from here."

Robin wanted to believe him. The lavish life that Lovely refused to live was something Robin wanted for herself. With Lovely's millions, Robin couldn't understand why Lovely chose to live a low-key lifestyle. Robin could only imagine the things she could do with money like Lovely's. And since Lovely wasn't going to divulge in it, why shouldn't Robin?

———

Ike sat on the sofa looking over the evidence he had before him. He was making sure Tomiko wasn't walking away from this marriage with anything. She was the one that decided to emotionally abandon the marriage and neglect him and the kids. And all for what? To fuck around? Tomiko was a classic hoe. She didn't know what having a good man meant. Ike had proven over the years that he was that good man. He gave her the world. He treated her kindly. He was sensitive to her needs. He loved her.

Melissa: you there?

Ike to Melissa: I'm here

Melissa: coming up

Ike smiled in anticipation of seeing Melissa again. He missed her so much. He was dying to get her voluptuous curvy body in his arms. He quickly gathered his photos and stuffed them back in the large clasp envelope.

Ike placed the envelope down as Melissa let herself in the condo. She stared at him for a second before walking towards him. She stripped herself of her coat and slung her purse on the back of the sofa that she passed. Ike didn't bother getting up from his seat. She placed one hand on her prominent hip and asked, "So why am I here?"

Ike reached out for her. "To see me, baby."

"Nuh uh," Melissa murmured knocking his hand away. "Who was that white bitch you had up in here?"

"Did you not listen to any of my voicemails or read any of the texts I sent?"

"I erased everything. You know I can't have that in my phone for too long. Reggie will see it."

Ike's face screwed up in an expression of disgust. He couldn't stand the sound of his name. "Fuck Reggie."

"Ike," Melissa said sternly.

"I can't stand his ass," he said. He asked, "Is he still acting stupid?"

"He has his moments."

Ike tried again. He reached out for her. "C'mere baby. I would never try to hurt you on purpose. Let me explain who the white woman was."

"I don't wanna hear some messed up lie Isaac."

Ike grinned at the sound of his legal name being used. "You won't. Everything is the truth."

Melissa allowed herself to be pulled into Ike's hold. He sat back pulling her with him forcing her to straddle his lap.

Ike whispered, "I miss you."

Melissa responded softly, "I miss you too."

"Show me how much you've missed me."

Melissa leaned in to give Ike a slow-paced sensual kiss on the lips. Ike returned the kiss' passion. His hands began to roam her upper body going under her shirt. He sucked and kissed on her neck working his way down to her clavicle. Against her skin, he whispered, "I want you so bad."

Melissa went for his pants. Ike asked with a teasing smile, "You don't wanna discuss the white woman first?"

Melissa shook her head as she freed his hard joystick from his boxers and pants. She grinned at him mischievously as she lowered her body down to be leveled with him. When Ike felt the wetness of Melissa mouth on him, he let his head fall back, and he closed his eyes. This was the attention he was definitely missing in his life.

Chapter Three

"What are you doing in my house?"

Those words awakened Abe. It felt like he had only been asleep thirty minutes but the brightness of the sun shining through the floor to ceiling windows let Abe know it was morning.

Abe looked up at his brother standing over him. "Why are you looking down at me like that?"

"Cause I didn't expect to see a big yella nigga in my guest room when I got home," Eli said. He folded his arms across his chest. "I'ma ask you again. Why are you in my home?"

Abe turned away from him. "Leave me alone Eli."

"You and Lovely had y'all first fight? Oh, how cute." Eli's tone was dry.

Abe didn't respond. It was just like his younger brother to make light of everything.

"I'm not leaving until you answer me," Eli said matter of factly. He sat down on the edge of the bed.

Abe looked over his shoulder at Eli. "Ain't that what you had on yesterday?"

Eli looked down at himself. "It is, but it ain't got shit to do with you being in my house."

"Where you been Eli?"

"Don't worry about that."

"Well, that's my answer to you too."

Eli rolled his eyes and mocked Abe. "Well, that's my answer—boy if you don't get your ass up! You got a company to run."

"Fuck that company," Abe mumbled.

"What?" Eli asked in shock. "Did I hear you right?"

"I'm not in the mood," Abe said. He turned around to face Eli. "I need some time off. Look at the schedule to make sure ain't nothing major happening in the next four weeks that will require my presence."

"Are you seriously going to take off from work like that?" Eli asked for clarification.

"I need to. I got a lot of shit on my mind that I need to sort out."

"Would it have to do with whatever Eric told you yesterday?"

"Maybe."

"It has something to do with Lovely. Is that why you're here and not over there with her?"

Abe nodded.

"But I thought you and Lovely were in love and couldn't nothing come in between that? Didn't you just ask Luciano and Cesar for her hand in marriage?"

39

Abe forgot about that. He left the ring in the closet. He was going to ask Lovely to marry him on Christmas. "Damn," he said under his breath.

———

Lovely feared the worst. Abe left. Now he was ignoring her calls. He had never done that. He always answered her calls, or he would return them quickly.

This was all wrong. This wasn't how it was supposed to be. Maybe she shouldn't have probed. She should have just let him have some space. She couldn't get over how he lacked enthusiasm over her being pregnant. Then on top of that, he stormed out and didn't bother returning home. If his mind was made up to walk away from their relationship, then she wouldn't force him to stay. She would let him go.

"What's wrong Lovely?" Robin asked.

Lovely looked in the direction of Robin's voice. "Nothing," she somberly said.

Robin joined her on the sofa. "Oh yes there is. Something is wrong with you. It's written all over your face. Do I need to get Abe for you?"

Lovely could hear that Robin was being playful, but Lovely wasn't amused. "Abe isn't here."

"I know. He should be at work, right?" Robin said.

"I don't know where he is," Lovely said sadly. "He's not answering my calls."

"Really?"

"Yeah," she said. "But I'm sure he's at work, and he's busy."

"You want me to call Eli?" Robin asked.

"No," Lovely said. Hoping to get her mind off of Abe, Lovely changed the subject by asking, "What's the deal with you and Eli?"

Robin smiled. "Nothing."

"Yeah right. You two have become really cozy with one another."

"We're getting closer," Robin said.

"How close?"

Robin whispered with excitement, "We had sex."

"What!" Lovely asked with surprise.

"Yeah and it was amazing," Robin said in a dreamlike faraway stare.

"Really? So...I mean...does that confirm for you that he's a straight man?" Lovely asked.

"Yeah, I guess. You know Eli's never said he was anything but straight anyway," Robin said. Her smiled faded and was replaced with a frown. "He didn't fuck like a gay man."

Lovely burst into laughter. "What does that mean?"

Robin chuckled too at what she said. "I mean, he seemed to really be into vagina."

"That's a good thing then."

"Yes," Robin said.

"I love Eli," Lovely said letting out a tickled sigh. "So, what about Mister Man?"

Robin knew Lovely was speaking of her married lover. Lowering her head, she said, "I saw him last night."

"Last night? I thought you were done with him."

Robin shrugged. "I wanna keep my options open. I'm sure Eli haven't cut none of his friends off."

Lovely waved her hand dismissively. "Girl, cut that man completely off."

"Well, I wanna still be his friend."

"Don't let it interfere with what you could have with Eli."

"I'm really not sure of what I could have with Eli."

"Shouldn't y'all be discussing that?" Lovely asked thinking of her own situation with Abe.

"Discuss? Eli ain't Abe," Robin said. "He's not all sensitive and shit."

"He really is. You just gotta deal with him a certain way to see that side of him," Lovely stated.

"Eli is difficult. Sometimes I wish I had hooked up with Abe instead."

Lovely's mouth dropped open. "Did you seriously just say that as if it was nothing?"

"I mean, I ain't hoping to be with your man or nothing," Robin said trying to correct what she had said. "It's just Abe is so fucking perfect."

"He ain't that perfect. He has flaws too," Lovely quickly countered. She smiled in thought. "But I appreciate every one of his flaws. He wouldn't be Abe without them."

Robin rolled her eyes, sick with Lovely's perfect perception on things.

Lovely's phone announced a call from Luciano. "Let me answer this."

"Okay. I'm headed to go see Eli anyway," Robin said as she headed out of the den.

Lovely answered on her earpiece device. "Hello?"

"Hey Lovely!"

"Hey Papa," Lovely smiled.

"How are things?" Luciano asked.

"They're good," she said. She felt as if she was lying because things weren't good. "How are you and your lovely wife?"

"Great. Listen, I was calling because I was coming down South to meet up with some business partners there in Nashville. Me and the missus would love to stop by and see you."

"Oh, come on. You're more than welcome to come by. I haven't seen you since Thanksgiving."

"Oh, I know. How's Abe?"

"He's good...I think."

"Oh-oh. Didn't like the sound of that," Luciano said.

"He's okay I guess. We kinda had a little quarrel, and he walked out last night. I haven't spoken to him since."

"Really?"

"Yeah. I'm not sure what he's going through, and usually, we can talk about anything. This is the first time he's actually shut down on me."

"Well did you tell him what you told me?"

"Yes. And that's what got me so boggled. He totally dismissed the news like it was no big deal."

"Abe? But having a baby is something he wants right?"

"It was," she sighed.

"Well give him a little space. He'll come around."

"Okay."

"How's Grace?"

"She's great. Still being crazy Grace though."

"Oh, will Jackie still be moving in?"

Lovely smiled at the mention of her younger cousin. "Yes, she will. She's excited, and you know Aunt Livy is too."

"Well, that's good. I guess I'll see you next week," Luciano said.

"Okay. Love you Papa Lu."

"*Ti amo amore mio.*"

Lovely ended the call. She pressed her Bluetooth device. "Call Abe."

It rung only to go to voicemail.

———

Robin called Eli as she drove through the black iron gates leaving Lovely's home. He answered on the second ring, "Hello?"

"Hey," Robin said sweetly.

"Hey," Eli said returning the sweetness.

"I didn't get my morning text."

"Oh, I know. I was busy and got distracted."

"Really? Abe working you like that?"

"Abe works the shit out of me always," Eli joked.

"Well can I come by and have lunch with you today?"

"I would say yes, but I'm not at the office today."

"You're not?"

"No. I'm at home."

Robin was just about to pass Magnolia Drive. She took a quick turn. "I'm coming to see you since I didn't get to see you last night."

"Well...I'm...kinda...," he said trying to come up with the right words.

"You're kinda nothing. I'm coming. I'll be there in two minutes. Bye." Robin ended the call. She laughed to herself.

When she pulled up to Eli's gate, it automatically opened for her. He had to be looking out for her.

She pulled up to the portico and noticed Abe's meteorite gray Aston Martin parked right in front of her. Robin frowned. He wasn't answering Lovely's calls, but he was at Eli's house. That didn't make any sense.

Before she could call Lovely, Eli's door swung open. He was standing there looking every bit of sexy. Robin smiled and got out of her car. "Hey."

"Come here lady," Eli ordered playfully. Robin walked up to him, and they shared a sweet, delicate kiss.

Robin looked up at him and pouted, "I missed you last night." This was a true statement despite Robin being with her lover.

"I missed you too. I wish you had come over," Eli said. He hoped the lie didn't show on his face.

"I should have," she said.

Eli stepped aside to let her in. He closed the door and followed her upstairs.

Robin asked looking around the corner, "Where's Abe? I see his car out there."

"He's laying down," Eli answered. He guided her towards his den.

"Is he sick?" she asked out of concern. "Lovely has been trying to get in touch with him. Is he drunk?"

"No, he just don't feel that well," Eli said. He asked, "Do you want me to get you something?"

"No, I'm fine," she said sitting down on the sofa.

Eli sat down beside her.

Robin said, "You know I've been thinking."

"About?"

"Us. What are we doing?"

"Right now, we're sitting on the sofa talking," he joked.

"No, you know what I'm talking about," she said.

"What are you asking?"

"Are we dating? Just fuck buddies? Go together?"

"What do you want Robin?"

She half shrugged.

"You know I have commitment issues," Eli said.

"I know. I'm glad you acknowledge you do."

"And I'm glad you made that observation as well."

46

Robin asked, "So are you bisexual? Is that why you have an issue with committing to me, a woman?"

Eli let out a slight laugh while shaking his head. "This shit again."

Robin said, "Eli, just tell me if you are or not."

"Damn! You don't know the answer to that already? I'm not—" he was saying when his buzzer interrupted him. Eli quickly switched his television to the security surveillance. His eyes widen, and he gasped. He quickly put the television back to the regular channel. "Let me take care of this real quick....Don't go nowhere. Sit right here."

Robin nodded, "Okay."

Eli went back down to his foyer and allowed the person access. He went outside to meet the car as it pulled up to the portico. Eli's brow was furrowed into a scowl. "What the hell are you doing here?"

"You left your wallet. It must've slipped out of your pants this morning," Kris said extending the wallet out to Eli. Kris' eyes shifted to Robin's car. "I see you have company."

"Kris, what did I just tell you about coming to my house?" Eli asked angrily. "You coulda just called me, and I would have come to get it. You didn't go through it, did you? All my shit better be in here. And I know how much cash I had."

Kris started laughing. "Really? I would never steal from you, Eli."

"I don't know. You hard headed as fuck," Eli said cutting his eyes at Kris.

Still wearing a playful smile, Kris said, "Oh don't worry. She won't suspect anything."

"That's not the point. My brother is here too."

Kris eyed the expensive luxury car. "So, I see."

Impatiently Eli said, "Okay, can you leave now?"

Kris hesitated, searching Eli's face. "I'm leaving."

"Okay. Go," he said.

"No, I'm leaving Eli...like leaving Nashville."

Eli frowned, "What do you mean?"

"I got a job offer in North Carolina," Kris said watching the disappointment settle over Eli. "I wasn't going to take it because of you...but you've shown me that I'm not what you really want. Even after last night. You were talking a lot of shit and apologizing, but I know if you had to do it all over again you'd be hiding me again for her."

Eli wasn't sure of what he should feel. He had always reminded Kris that what they had was a fuck thing that didn't need to be up for public knowledge. However, Eli was feeling fucked up about Kris' news. "When are you leaving?"

"Today. I wanted to tell you before you left this morning, but I was having second thoughts about leaving. But I know this is what's best for me...and you."

"How can you determine what's best for me?" Eli asked, feeling the anger grow from within.

"Okay, I can't speak for you," Kris said putting the car's gear in reverse. Kris looked out of the window at Eli. "I won't hold you up any longer."

"Why are you just now telling me this? Damn, you didn't even put in a two weeks' notice. You could have at least done that so they could find someone to replace you."

"My decision came suddenly."

"Whatever Kris," Eli said cutting his eyes.

She didn't know what else to say. They stared at each other. Kris could see the apparent irritation on Eli's face. Kris finally said, "I love you, Eli."

"Fuck you," Eli spat as he turned to go back to his front door. He didn't bother looking back when he closed the door behind him. He took a few seconds to compose himself. Hearing that Kris was leaving him had Eli vexed.

When Eli made it back upstairs, Robin was still sitting in the spot he had left her. Abe was now in the den looking a bit more refreshed.

Abe asked, "Who was that?"

In his true form, Eli exaggerated a grimace and said, "None of your business. That's why I don't like people at my house."

"Uhm...technically this is still my house. I could put you out," Abe chuckled.

Robin looked over at Abe, "So are you going to call Lovely? She seemed a little off when I left her."

"I will. I am," Abe said heading into the kitchen.

"Good," Robin said. Her eyes lingered on Abe's physique. She could feel Eli's gaze on her. She looked at Eli and smiled, "I was sitting here thinking."

"Isn't that always," Eli said dryly. He made a mental note about the way Robin had looked too long at Abe. Something didn't sit right with Eli with that.

"Don't be getting smart," Robin threatened with playfulness. She looked at Eli long and smiled.

"What?" Eli asked wondering what the hell she was smiling about.

"Nothing. So where do you want to take this?" she asked.

Eli wasn't in the mood to discuss him and Robin. He wanted to get on the phone and cuss Kris out, then turn around and ask Kris not to leave. He said, "I know I'm not ready for anything exclusive."

Robin said, "Well we can take things slow."

"Sounds good to me," Eli said lacking enthusiasm.

With concern, Robin asked, "Are you okay?"

Eli turned to her and forced a small smile, "I'm fine."

Eli was far from fine. In that moment he realized that his feelings for Kris were deeper than what he thought.

Chapter Four

D avid was Abe's confidant, his mentor, and his friend. Whenever life became too much for Abe to deal with he ran right to David. David's son Troy used to be Abe's best friend. He was killed years ago. Abe always felt like it was his place to be somewhat of the son David had lost.

Abe found himself headed over to David's place of business during lunch. Since Eli was badgering Abe to tell him what was going on, Abe insisted Eli and Ike tag along, and he could explain to all three of them at the same time.

Abe spotted David immediately when they entered the restaurant. Abe went up to him with desperation etched on his face. He asked, "David, can I talk with you for a second?"

David looked up at the three brothers, "Of course."

David led them to the privacy of his back office. He made sure he shut both sets of doors.

Seeing the troubled expression on Abe's face, David asked, "What is it, Abe? You look troubled. Is there anything I can do to help?"

"It must be something really bad," Eli murmured.

David's eyes shifted to Eli. "You don't know what's wrong with him either?"

Eli shook his head.

Ike mumbled, "I don't either."

Abe looked at each man. "It really is bad."

Eli stared back at Abe. He was waiting on Abe to disclose the secret. When Abe didn't say anything, Eli asked, "Did you cheat on Lovely?"

"My life is about to go to shit," Abe said rubbing his hands over his head in a bothered way.

David chuckled, "Because you cheated or something on Lovely?"

"No. I wished I had. It would be simpler," Abe said.

"What the fuck did you do?" Eli chuckled.

"It's not funny Eli," Ike said cutting his eyes at Eli.

"Sorry but hell if cheating is better than this then damn," Eli said.

"Listen," he began but was cut off by his phone ringing. Quickly he glanced at his phone's display. It was Lovely. He couldn't answer it just yet. "That's Lovely."

"You're not gonna talk to her?" Eli asked.

"I can't," he said shaking his head. He looked over at Ike, Eli, and David with despair and sorrow. "This stays between us."

Eli looked at him incredulously, "Who are we gonna tell Abe?"

Abe knew he could trust his brothers. As children, they had been through a lot that kept their bond tight. Uneasiness settled over him as he prepared to let the words out. "I was involved in what happened to Lovely."

"What about her?" David asked.

Carefully, Abe replied, "I kinda knew of her parents."

David waited for Abe to continue. "Okay..."

Abe sighed in exasperation. "David, this is one of the most fucked up situations I've ever found myself in."

"Will you get to it!" David urged.

"Lovely didn't have some accident that caused her visual impairment. She was shot in the head," Abe explained in a sullen tone.

Eli gasped. "And you did it? But..."

David look to Abe to see if he was going to confirm where Eli was going with this.

Abe looked David in the eyes and said, "Lovely is the daughter of a couple I helped to rob and...kill."

David was completely thrown. He had to have a seat. "What?"

"David you knew what I was doing out there in the streets," Abe said. He walked over to the picture window and gazed out into the back courtyard.

"I know but Abe...my God," David said shaking his head.

Eli turned away from Abe feeling sick. Now he understood his brother's devastation. He asked, "Why?"

"Money. It was the last thing I did. Hell, I still got money from that I hadn't touched. I didn't pull the trigger that shot Lovely. But I ordered it though," he said. All of the guilt and shame returned. He shook his head, "I can't be with her knowing what I did."

"Abe," Eli whispered, devastated and in shock. "How? Why? How long you been knowing this?"

"Yesterday. Eric told me who Lovely was."

"Let me guess; Eric was right there with you when all this happened?" Ike asked.

"Him and Lorenzo. Lorenzo raped and shot Lovely. I believe—No, I know Grace is Lorenzo's daughter," Abe said.

"This happened all in one day?" David asked, still trying to receive all of this news.

Abe hung his head in shame. "It all happened when we robbed Lovely's father."

David's devastation was just as deep as Abe's. He knew Abe's past. Time after time David would lecture his son and Abe about being in the street. He knew Abe was so much more than the illegal activities he used to be involved in. And once Abe got tired of the streets he proved that by going to school and earning not one but three degrees in his line of business. He had taken illegal money and invested in his company to produce legit money. David had been so proud of Abe. But this news was a big blow to Abe's present character.

"How much did y'all get out of it? I mean was it worth it?" Ike wanted to know.

"Millions," Abe replied.

"What?" Eli was stunned.

Abe continued on. "For doing the job I kept a nice portion of it. Antino got his cut and the rest was split between Eric and Lorenzo."

"Antino?" Both Eli and David asked at the same time. Both were just as shocked because that was a name Abe hadn't spoken of in years.

Abe nodded, "He's the one that called on my help."

"You mean Antino the one you used to work for?" David asked for clarity.

"Yeah," Abe murmured.

Giving it some thought, Eli asked, "Lovely was supposed to die, right?"

"She should have been dead," Abe stated.

"Antino and Lo; how do you think they will feel about her being alive?" Ike asked.

Abe hadn't given that much thought. Would they react the same way Eric had and want to finish her off? He couldn't let that happen.

"What are you gonna do Abe?" David finally asked.

Abe shook his head emphatically, "I can't tell Lovely the truth. Not now at least."

David folded his arms and leaned back in his chair. "Let me ask you this Abe. Are you with Lovely because of the guilt?"

"No. I love Lovely. I bought a ring with the intention to propose on Christmas before I even realized who she was. I was gonna ask her to marry me, and we would be engaged for a few months while she planned the wedding of her dreams. I'm deeply in love with Lovely. But the guilt is getting to me."

"How do you think she will feel once she finds out the truth? Would you want her to forgive you and move on?" David asked.

"I would, but I know that's not realistic. She will hate me," Abe said.

"She might, but you would hope she wouldn't," David said.

"Then I don't know what Kiera has up her sleeve. I mean I know that's your niece, but I don't know if I can trust her to be quiet. She messy as hell David," Abe stated.

David chuckled, "But wasn't she like that years ago?"

Abe said, "I expected for her to have grown up a little. She was all right when she first moved in."

David sighed, "Don't fall victim to what the devil wants out of you. For the past what, ten years you've been doing a great job holding up and being the upstanding man you are. Don't let all those years of you turning your life around be in vain Abe."

Abe turned to David, Ike, and Eli and asked, "Okay so what about Lovely. How do I handle that?"

"Tell her the truth," David simply said.

Abe's eyes widen. "Are you crazy?"

"No. Do you think she'll be quick to leave you when she finds out?" David queried.

Abe stepped away from the window. "You don't know Lovely. She'll snap on me in a minute and tell me she doesn't need me. She already told me I could leave."

David laughed. "Little Lovely?"

"Don't let her innocent face fool you," Abe said.

Eli said, "Well you can't keep avoiding her without a reasonable explanation."

"I know," Abe said with a sigh. "I just wished that I could love her, make her my wife and hopefully when she learns the truth she'll love me so much she'll be willing to forgive me and leave all of that in the past."

"Abe, that's not realistic though," Ike said.

"Damn Ike! Let me have this. Please!" Abe exclaimed.

Ike threw his hands up in surrender. "Okay, I'll shut up."

"You wanna know what I think you should do?" Eli asked.

"Not really," Abe said flatly.

Eli was going to tell him anyway. "Don't run from Lovely. You owe her Abe. The least you can do is make it up to her by loving her. Go ahead and marry her like you planned to do so. And maybe just maybe if and when she learns the truth she'll love you so much she'll forgive you."

"I was involved in killing her parents!" Abe exclaimed. "She will not forgive me no matter what I do. She'll probably have me thrown in prison."

"She doesn't have to ever know," Eli reasoned.

David stood up and joined at his side. "Son, I know this is difficult for you but prepare yourself for the worst. Everything done in the dark will come to light. She will learn the truth one day, and it won't be nothing you can do to stop it."

Abe sighed with grief. He looked David in his eyes. He sadly said, "Then there's the fact that she's pregnant."

A smile lit David's face. "That's a good thing. You've always wanted your own little family."

"Yeah but with this other shit...," his voice trailed as he thought about the situation. "I don't know what to do. I don't know how to feel. Do I even have a right to be with her?"

David answered with a slight shrug of the shoulders, "The past is the past. The two of you share a very special kind of love. It glows around y'all like some type of halo. I see it. I'm sure what y'all have is worth the risk."

Thoughts of Lovely flooded Abe's mind. There was no denying that he truly loved her.

"I know you left yesterday after she told you she was pregnant but have y'all had the time to talk about it since?" David asked.

Abe shook his head. "No. I think she thinks I've been acting like an ass because I've been avoiding her. I left again last night and went to Eli's."

"Well stop acting like a damn ass and be the man I know you can be to her," David said with an encouraging smile.

Abe exhaled heavily. "I am."

Sympathetically David said, "Abe I hate that you're going through this. You were doing so good."

"I'm still doing good, David. It's just...I can't let Lovely know this. Not yet. Maybe after she have the baby," Abe said as his mind went into deep thought. As far as Abe was truly concerned, Lovely would never hear of what he had done.

––––––––

The time in the lower right corner of his monitor read 7:09 pm. Abe had been in his office late enough. He was actually bored; his current project didn't hold his interest. It was his proposed designs for Luciano's BevyCo World Wide Resorts next location there in Tennessee. As complex as it was, it wasn't enough to distract his mind from what was really bothering him.

Two days had passed since the past had reared its ugly head. Abe's friend Eric had come and snatched any joy Abe had been feeling by exposing who Lovely really was. Abe was genuinely happy with his newfound life with Lovely and her daughter Grace. Now he had to face the fact that he had been part of the ugliness that scarred Lovely for life, physically and psychologically.

To cope, Abe had worked long hours and had been drinking. He couldn't stand himself to even be blessed by Lovely's presence. Even during this time while he distanced himself from Lovely, she remained loving and understanding. Not once did she confront him or give him any static about the cold shoulder he had given her. After the first day of not answering his phone or returning his call, Lovely stopped calling him after she left him one lone message.

"Hey, Abe baby. I get it...You really wanted your space. I won't bother you anymore after this...I'll respect your needs. I'd hate for you to resent me. So, you take as long as you need. When you're ready, I'll be here. I love you."

This was the third day he had kept his distance from her. He couldn't stand being away from Lovely any longer. Besides he needed to show her his excitement and happiness over the pregnancy.

Abe called Eli to let him know he was going to Lovely's and not to expect him.

"About time nigga," Eli said. "I was on the verge of putting your ass out. For real."

"Shut up. How many times I gotta tell you that house still belong to me. I could put you out," Abe said as his second line beeped. "Hey Eli, I got another call. Let me holla at you later."

"Okay."

Abe answered the other line. "Hello?"

"What's up nigga?" Eric said into the phone.

"What's up?" Abe replied. He felt a little guilty and remorseful for hitting Eric the way he had Sunday.

"I was just calling to check on ya. I hadn't heard from you."

"That's because I've been trying to deal with this shit. Man, this some tough shit to swallow."

"I know it is."

"Ay look, man, I'm sorry for hitting you like that. My emotions were just all over the place."

"You straight. I understand. But had it been some regular ass nigga he would have gotten the business."

"I know. So, you back in Richmond?"

"Yeah...But I think it's time for me to relocate."

"You're doing it now?"

"Yeah. We coming when the kids' winter break starts so she can have them enrolled in school down there when school start back."

"Oh."

"Besides my auntie and mama live there. It's time for me to return to my roots."

"Good. We can do business easier," Abe said. "Let me know when you'll be here so we can get together."

"Will do," Eric said.

"A'ight nigga. Get off my phone."

Eric chuckled, "Bye yella mothafucka."

Abe ended the call just as he was pulling up to Lovely's. He entered the code to gain access. The gates opened. He drove up the winding driveway and didn't bother parking in the garage. He pulled up along the front door. Feeling eager at first, he suddenly felt uneasy. He hoped Lovely was truly an understanding person and wouldn't give him too much resistance.

Going into the house, he immediately went to the bedroom despite the laughter and voices soaring in from the family room. It didn't surprise him much when he saw Lovely in bed propped up against plush pillows. She was using the remote to the television until she noticed him walk in. Her arm dropped, and her eyes locked on him. "Abe?"

"Yeah," he said. He walked over to the bed noticing that his side was left undisturbed.

"You here to get your stuff?" she asked. Her voice came out small and soft.

"No," he said. He looked at her full breast and her erect nipples pressed against the thin cotton fabric of the pink racerback night tee she was wearing. Her hair was growing wildly. Big loose curls hung over her left eye. Abe kicked off his shoes and crawled in the bed towards her. He pushed her hair off her face. "Are you growing your hair?"

"Yeah," she said. Her eyes were darting all over his face. She was trying to see him.

Abe brought his face to hers but paused before kissing her. He looked at her loving face and her innocent eyes searching his face. She couldn't make out his face, but she always tried as if her vision would change. God, he hated what he had done. Abe kissed her on the forehead. "I miss you."

It seemed as if Lovely had stopped breathing. Having Abe that close to her had taken her breath away. She wanted to touch him. She wanted to attack him with kisses and hugs, but she would play it cool. "I miss you too. And I'm sorry for coming at you like that."

"No need to apologize. I was the one acting crazy."

"I know, but I didn't make matters any better. I'm so sorry, and you know I don't want you to leave," she said desperately.

Abe put a soft sweet kiss on her nose. "If I told you I'll never leave you again would you believe me?"

Lovely nodded.

"Good. Because I'm not," he said. He kissed her lips sensually and slow, sucking her bottom lip. He coaxed her into lying down where he proceeded to remove her panties from under her night tee.

Lying down with his head in between her legs Abe began to make love to her with his tongue. Lovely exhaled with relief as the tension escaped her body. She closed her eyes and enjoyed the way his tongue caressed every fold of her slit making sure to tease her bliss button. "Baby...," she moaned as his tongue went in and out of her causing her to flow with more nectar for him to feed upon.

Lovely began rocking her hips back and forward. She grabbed his head and started thrusting herself against his now stiffened tongue. He allowed her to navigate where his tongue went. She moved so that it was back on her clit and she moved in circular motions on it. He finally had enough, so he threw her hands away from his head. He wanted to make her cum. Over and over he beat her clit up with his tongue flickering it up and down.

Lovely's scream came from nowhere, and her body tensed up as she exploded without warning. "Oh my God!" she groaned.

Abe moved on top of her kissing her on the lips and neck as he grinded his hardness against her still sensitive love pot. Lovely returned the grind. She needed to feel him inside her. He wanted to feel her. His dick was going to bust through his pants.

"Please Abe," Lovely begged as she wrestled with the buckle of his belt.

"Please what?" he asked toying with her.

"I need to feel you, baby," Lovely said desperately.

"How bad?"

"Bad."

"Do you love me?"

"Yes!"

"How much?"

"A lot. C'mon stop playing," she whined impatiently.

Abe removed his shirt and ribbed tank. Then he removed his jeans and boxers. Lovely practically pulled him into her.

Too much at once caused her to cry out in pleasure laced with a feel so good pain.

Softly whispering against her lips, he said, *"Te quiero tanto mi amor."*

No matter how many times they made love, it always felt like the first time. His girth filled her and stretched her to capacity every time. Lovely felt sorry for the man to follow him. That was an amusing thought. Lovely never had a thought of another man coming after Abe.

He continued to whisper sweet nothings in her ear in Spanish as he stroked her long and slow. It was one of those torturous slow strokes that made her quiver and thrust on his dick wanting more. He was being methodical and deliberate massaging her g-spot with the thickness of him. Abe knew exactly what he was doing. He knew what would get her there. Lovely cried tears as she had an explosive back to back orgasm that resulted in her gushing. Abe loved when she did that. He would pull back and just watch her body jerk and twitch.

Not saying anything Abe simply kissed the stream of tears rolling down Lovely's face. She buried her face in his neck as he continued to stroke her at a faster pace. Whenever he went deeper, she would gently bite his neck. He loved it when she nibbled at him. It only made him go deeper.

The way he made love to her was very emotional and fervent. He wanted her to know how sorry he was about the past. He apologized with every stroke. He held her close and kissed her all over tenderly. After they both climaxed simultaneously, Abe held her tightly.

Listening to the rhythm of his deep breathing, Lovely let sleep take over.

Abe admired Lovely's beauty as he watched her sleep. All he could think of was how could he erase the past and restore her vision. He could love her. He could provide her a love like no other. That's what he would do. Simply love her.

———

As the days went by and Christmas neared Abe found himself more relaxed. Lovely made it so easy for him. She was the most loving affectionate woman he had ever been with. His conscience almost wouldn't let him be with her. But he loved the shit out of Lovely. She was carrying his child. What could be more beautiful than that? But there was still the issue of Grace. Abe always thought Grace resembled the Masters. Now it was obvious that Grace was definitely Lorenzo's child. That fact pissed Abe off even more about the fucked-up position he was in.

Lovely placed her hand on Abe's bouncing knee. "Baby, are you all right?"

Abe covered her hand with his and intertwined his fingers with hers. He brought her hand up to his mouth and kissed the back of it. "I'm fine."

"You seem anxious. Are you nervous?" Lovely asked.

They sat in the doctor's office waiting to be seen by Dr. Bradshaw. This would be Lovely's first prenatal visit. Abe wanted to be there for everything every step of the way concerning her pregnancy.

"Ms. Prasad!"

Lovely and Abe got up to follow the assistant to the back. Abe waited quietly and patiently as the medical assistant took Lovely through all of the routine checks. He felt the other staff and some patients ogling him, but he didn't pay them much attention. It was the same stares and delighted smiles he got whenever he was around women. He wondered if Lovely could see these women's faces if she would have a problem with it. Would she be jealous and say something? Lovely really didn't come off as the insecure type. Abe was a little territorial though. He didn't like when men gawked at Lovely, and it was quite often.

The medical assistant led them to an exam room and ordered Lovely to undress from the waist down. Once the medical assistant left them alone, Abe asked, "Is he gonna look up in your pussy with me in here?"

Lovely giggled. "Yes, unless it's uncomfortable for you then you can go outside for that part of the exam."

"Nah. I'm not leaving. I'm sitting in here and watching his ass. Make sure he ain't tryna play in my pussy," Abe said.

Lovely laughed. "You're crazy." She eased up on the exam table and placed the cloth sheet over her lap. Abe stood in front of her and wrapped his arms around her and kissed her on the forehead.

He said, "I've been thinking...we should get married."

Lovely asked, "And how long have you been thinking that?"

"Honestly?"

"Yeah."

"Since the day I laid eyes on you."

Lovely rolled her eyes with a grin. "You're so cheesy, Abe."

"Yeah for you. I'll be a cheeseball all damn day."

"And that's why I love you," Lovely said sweetly.

"I love you too baby. So, what do you think?"

"About the marriage thing?"

"Yes. How do you feel about it? I could adopt Grace as my own."

Lovely laughed lightly. "Is this a proposal?"

Abe was about to reply but was interrupted by a knock at the door. Lovely called out, "Come in."

Dr. Bradshaw and his nurse Veronica stepped into the patient examination room wearing big grins. Dr. Bradshaw said, "Well you ready to hear the news?"

Lovely could tell from his upbeat tone that he was about to tell her something that she already knew. She said cheerfully wearing a big grin, "I'm pregnant."

"You must certainly are," Dr. Bradshaw stated. He looked toward Abe and extended his hand. "I'm assuming you're proud papa."

Abe shook his hand. "That would be me."

Dr. Bradshaw, who was a nice height himself took in Abe's presence fully. "You're a big guy. I can only imagine what this baby gon' be like."

Lovely snickered. She said, "I don't wanna give birth to no giants."

"I delivered a ten pounder the other day. Baby look like he was already three months old," Dr. Bradshaw chuckled.

Abe watched Dr. Bradshaw glove his hands. He ordered Lovely to lay back and put her feet in the stirrups. When he proceeded to examine Lovely, she winced slightly. Abe said, "Please don't hurt my woman doc."

Dr. Bradshaw wore an amused smile as his hand was still inside of Lovely. The smirk on his face told Abe that his hand could do no more damage to Lovely than Abe's dick could do.

Lovely said, "Abe, he's not hurting me. Will you relax? You're more anxious than I am."

Dr. Bradshaw laughed. "I get fathers in here all the time that feel a need to be protective. Consider yourself one of the lucky ones because you have a husband that cares. However, it can be awkward at times." He pressed around on her stomach. "Yeah, you're good and pregnant." He took some measurements and frowned. "When was your last cycle?"

"About two and half weeks ago but I'm very irregular," Lovely said.

Dr. Bradshaw squeezed some warm gel over Lovely's belly and began moving the Doppler over it. He chuckled and was delighted at the sound of the fetus' rapid heartbeat. "I'm gonna have to send you for an ultrasound because you're definitely more than two weeks pregnant. You hear that? That's your junior."

Lovely smiled with delight and excitement. Her bright, goofy smile made Abe chuckle.

"You're measuring about eleven weeks. But according to you, your last menstrual was two and half weeks ago. An ultrasound will give us a more accurate gestational age."

"When can I get one?" Lovely asked eagerly.

"We can probably get you back in here by early next week," he said.

Abe asked, "Is there something wrong?"

"No, not at all. Veronica, show them to my office after she gets dressed. Mr. Prasad, I'll go over everything th—"

"Masters," Abe corrected. "It's Abe Masters."

"Masters?" Dr. Bradshaw said with thought. He asked, "You wouldn't happen to be related to the owner of Masters Construction?"

Abe said, "I am the owner of Masters Construction."

Dr. Bradshaw smiled, "My daughter just purchased one of those Germantown condos your company built. Absolutely gorgeous."

"Thanks," Abe smiled modestly.

"Your company does outstanding work," Dr. Bradshaw said. He smiled and said, "Well I'll see you two in a little bit."

When Dr. Bradshaw and Veronica were gone, Abe asked Lovely, "Are you okay?"

"Are you gonna be like this every single time?" Lovely asked with a smile.

"I just wanna make sure you don't hurt or anything. That's my baby you're carrying in there. I need to make sure both of you are okay. Always."

Lovely said with a teasing smile, "You're really sweet. You know that?"

Yeah, Abe thought with derision. She had no idea. He said, "I'm supposed to be. Would you want me any other way?"

"Of course not. You're the best."

———

Later that night as they prepared for bed, Abe brought the subject of marriage up again. He told Lovely, "You can have the wedding of your dreams."

"How soon are you talking Abe?" Lovely asked.

"As soon as you get the plans together."

Lovely gave it some thought and said, "Well we can just wait 'til after I have the baby."

"Nonsense," Abe countered.

"I don't wanna walk down the aisle with a big ol' pregnant belly."

"Well, you're not having this baby without being Mrs. Abram Masters."

Lovely smiled. "Okay. How about we get married now. Nothing fancy. Very small and private. Then after I have the baby on our anniversary, we have a wedding."

Abe grinned. "Are you saying you wanna marry me Lovely?"

Lovely chuckled. "I am."

"Are you sure?"

Lovely nodded. "I'm positive."

The idea of a child began to warm Abe. He smiled. "What do you want?"

"What are you talking about?"

"The baby. What sex do you want it to be?"

"I guess it doesn't' matter as long as it's healthy."

"Yeah, yeah, yeah. I don't want the Miss America answer. What do you really want?"

Lovely smiled and said, "A boy."

"I do too but if it's a girl that'll be fine too," Abe said. He placed his hand on her belly and said, "I'm about to be a daddy."

"Does that make you happy?"

Her smile made him smile. "It does."

————

Four months of only knowing one another was a bit scary for Lovely, but her gut told her everything was fine. With so much monetary value between them, they thought it wise for both of them to sign prenuptial agreements. Money was the furthest thing from Abe's mind though. He was so guilty inside that it was okay if she took all he had. No material thing or any amount of money could be enough to repay what he helped to take from her twelve years ago.

After a very festive holiday, Lovely became Mrs. Abram Masters. This was a time where she wished her parents were still alive. It saddened her every time she celebrated something as joyous as this, and they were not around.

"Baby what's wrong?" Abe asked her. Lovely sat quietly at the bar in Abe's lower level man cave. Everyone else around them was being boisterous and loud. It was a celebration, but Lovely didn't seem to be into it. Abe asked, "Are you not feeling good?"

"I feel fine," she stated rubbing her curved out belly. She forced a small smile. "I'm just a little sad. I wish my parents were here."

Fuck! Abe thought. Of course, she would. This was a special day. He said, "I wish they were here for you too. I wish

71

I could have met them to thank them for producing such a lovely lady."

Lovely's smile widened. "My mama would have loved you. My daddy probably not so much. He was really protective, and he used to say I couldn't date until I was thirty."

"I feel the same way about Grace," he said looking across the room at the lanky pre-teen. He really wished Grace could have been his child instead of Lorenzo's. The good thing about it was Grace definitely had kind ways like her mother.

"I don't think Grace will be into boys until she's thirty," Lovely joked.

Abe caressed Lovely's face with the back of his hand. Lovely moved her face into his hand as if she was a cat being rubbed. She smiled, "I love when you do that."

"I know. Go ahead and purr like a cat," he teased.

Lovely made him laugh when she started purring. He said, "You're so silly. Was that all that was bothering you?"

"Well I'm a little anxious about having this baby," she said.

"Why?"

She shrugged as tears came to her eyes. Abe became worried. "Baby don't cry. You and the baby will be fine. You'll have as much help as you need."

Tears ran down either cheek. "That's not what I'm upset about."

Luciano and his wife Cece walked over to where Lovely and Abe were. Luciano was smiling until he saw Lovely's tear-streaked face. "What's the matter? Abe, she hadn't been your wife a full twenty-four hours and you already making her cry."

"It's not me," Abe said. He pulled Lovely close to him. "What is it, baby?"

Kiera asked, "What's wrong with Lovely?"

Lovely smiled through her tears, "I'm all right. I'm just having a moment."

"Ah," Cece crooned as she gazed upon Lovely and Abe. "I just love them together."

Abe asked Lovely, "Are you gonna tell me what's the matter?"

"It's just I'm about to have yet another baby whose face I will never be able to see," Lovely said.

Abe felt like shit. Why on this day, the day that Abe made Lovely his wife did he have to be reminded of the things that happened to Lovely?

———

Ike was truly happy for his brother, but it pained him to know that his brother was harboring such a deep secret that could destroy what he had with Lovely. For Abe's sake, Ike hoped Lovely never found out the truth. But keeping secrets were such a hurtful thing. Looking over at Melissa, Ike knew of that all too well.

Melissa turned to Ike and smiled, "Lovely's gonna be so cute pregnant. But isn't that sweet though."

"Yeah, it is. It's what Abe wanted. I'm glad to see him happy," Ike said. He looked at Melissa and said, "I wished you had been pregnant."

"We're not going to go there," Melissa sighed.

"Lissa, why you treating me like this? What have I done wrong?"

"I just don't wanna leave one mess and get into another one," she said.

"So, I'm a mess?"

Melissa didn't answer.

Ike nodded acknowledging her silent reply. "Okay. So, do you wanna talk about Tabitha now?"

Melissa shrugged.

"And I guess you don't believe me about Tabitha?"

"I believe you. So, are you going to go through with a divorce?"

"Yeah. I'm not doing any of this for nothing. I'm ready to move on. I was hoping I could with you."

"I don't think that's what I'm ready for."

"Well, what about my son?"

"What about him?"

"I wanna be with him on a regular basis."

"I'll think about it."

Ike asked, "So where is Reggie anyway? Shouldn't you be somewhere under him instead of over here?"

Melissa shrugged.

Ike said, "I wonder where Tomiko's ass is. She's probably meeting with Reggie right now."

"Ike, you've been drinking baby," Melissa said sweetly. She got up to walk away. She wasn't trying to hear what Ike was insinuating.

Ike was right behind her following her to the empty dining room. He walked up on her and pulled her to him. She pushed away, but he held tighter.

"Let me go," she fussed struggling to get away. He grabbed the back of her neck and pulled her forward so that he could kiss her. Melissa turned her face. He kissed her neck instead.

"Stop Ike."

"You stop fighting."

She stopped moving in his arms. "I don't want to do this with you."

"I don't care," he whispered. He kissed her neck again.

"You should," she said growing weak under his kisses.

Ike felt her defenses diminish. He kissed her on the lips passionately. Melissa returned the kiss with the same passion. Ike pulled away to ask, "Can I have you?"

"Now?" Melissa asked.

"I'm not talking about sex."

Melissa looked away from his piercing gaze. "What then?"

"All of you. I want you. I don't wanna keep making the same mistake. I want you to be with me, Melissa."

"Ike you don't want me."

"I do. I did."

"You were trying to make things work with Tomiko at first."

"No. I gave her that impression so that she could feel comfortable doing what she was doing. I needed a lot of good evidence because I absolutely don't want her walking away with anything."

"Okay so why didn't you tell me that?"

Ike said, "If I had told you, you probably would have wanted to know everything. I don't wanna speak on it because I didn't want Tomiko alluding to anything I was doing. Then I didn't want you thinking I was hooking up with you because of payback."

"But I accused you of it anyway. So, what was the difference?"

"Tabitha, the white lady at the condo and her partner Aaron are private investigators that I hired to take pictures of Tomiko with about four different men over the past four months. I have video too. Kissing, touching, hugging, cars parked outside of hotels, holding hands at different places, having dinner, at the mall...Tomiko was a hoe."

Melissa was confused. "So why didn't you just tell me this Ike?"

Ike shrugged. Seeing Jackie walk in the den wearing a fitted winter white dress that hugged her every curve. He had to admit that Jackie had been quite a distraction during the ceremony earlier. Ike had to do a double take. He could definitely tell Jackie was related to Lovely. Jackie had hips for days and a nice shapely plump ass.

"I promise I'll be out in five seconds," Jackie said sheepishly as she headed for the array of catered food lining the dining room table.

Melissa looked up at Ike and caught his eyes lingering on Jackie's ass. Typical man. Melissa said, "I gotta go and see about my husband." She grabbed chocolate truffle from the table and headed towards the foyer.

Jackie walked upon Ike. "You got a thing for her huh?"

He flashed her a smile of amusement. How much have she been paying attention to them? "Why do you say that?"

"I'm a people watcher," she answered. "I see things."

"Oh, I was beginning to think you were just watching me," Ike flirted.

Jackie blushed. "You need to stop."

Ike smiled, "You are kinda cute though."

"Kinda? Thanks a lot," Jackie said with feigned insult.

He asked, "How come I don't see you talking to anybody?"

"There's no one I'm interested in," she said.

"But I'm sure you got plenty of men after you."

"Not really. I don't really go anywhere like the clubs or nothing. I'm mostly around y'all. Me and Lovely get hollered at all the time, but they don't be my type of guy," Jackie explained.

"What's your type of guy?"

Jackie began to walk away. She threw over her shoulder in an alluring manner, "You."

Ike smiled as he roused to attention. "Where you going?"

"To my room," she said while continuing to walk.

Ike was hypnotized by the jiggle of her ass and the bounce of her breasts. He said, "Jackie, why don't you stay out here with me for a little bit."

Chapter Five

About a week after Abe and Lovely exchanged vows, Kiera decided that she should go and have a little talk with Abe. He was in good spirits, and Kiera definitely needed to take advantage of it. She found herself at Abe's place of business, but before getting to Abe, she had to mess with Eli.

"I really don't have time for your fuckery today. Furthermore, I am not in the mood," Eli was saying to Kiera. She had sat on the other side of Eli's desk and was bothering him as she always had.

Kiera smiled, "I see that."

"Get that smile off your face," Eli said.

She lowered her voice, "You want me, don't you?"

"I do?" he asked sarcastically.

"Are you still seeing Robin?"

Eli looked into Kiera's eyes. "Why?"

"Cause I wanna see you. Fuck that bitch. She can't do for you the way I can."

Eli shook his head at Kiera wearing an amused smile. "Yeah, well...," he said as he heard the softness of a familiar voice. It was Robin. What was she doing here?

"Hey, you," Robin said standing in Eli's cubicle entrance. She was smiling even as she looked down at Kiera.

Eli smiled, "Hey. What are you doing here?"

"I'm here to see you," Robin said with a bright smile.

"Have you had lunch?" Eli asked. He had completely forgotten about Kiera who was sitting back quietly and watching them.

Robin shook her head. "I was just about to ask you that?"

"Well we can do that together," Eli said. He joined Robin in the waiting area totally disregarding Kiera's presence.

Kiera rolled her eyes. Eli couldn't seriously be into that pale skin bitch. There was something about Robin that Kiera couldn't seem to get past. Kiera knew she herself was known for being messy, but that damn Robin was a sneaky bitch. Kiera was sure of it.

She looked towards Abe's office door just as he was seeing someone out. This was her opportunity to walk in there. He disappeared back inside but left his door opened. Kiera went to his door and gave a light tap, "Knock, knock."

Abe looked up, and a frown immediately covered his face.

Kiera said, "Abe, I need to talk to you about something."

Abe turned his attention back to his computer monitor. His annoyed state shown on his face. He prepared himself for Kiera's bullshit. He said, "Shut the door please."

Kiera shut the door then sat down in a chair on the other side of his desk. "I'm glad you were willing to talk to me."

Still not looking at her, he asked, "What can I do for you, Kiera?"

"I need an investor. And you're perfect for this."

Abe finally looked at her and asked, "I am?"

Kiera grinned. "Yes!"

"How so?"

"Because you have the money. And I heard you invest in black businesses all of the time."

"I do. I'm always open to investing in the empowerment of our people within our own community. But why should I invest in you?"

Kiera sighed. "Look I'm not trying to come at you wrong or nothing like that. But I would really like this salon."

Abe sat back in his chair eyeing Kiera with an intense stare. "Again, why should I invest in you?"

Kiera looked him dead on. "I just figured if you do this favor for me I could help you keep your secret a secret."

"So, in order words, you're blackmailing me?" Abe asked with amusement.

"I just wanna do business with you. So, can you help me out or what?"

Abe asked, "So if I decide I don't want to do business with you, you're going to tell on me?"

Kiera shrugged with uncertainty. Abe narrowed his eyes at her. His eyes appeared icy and cold. A chill ran down her spine that made her squirm in her seat. She looked away from his stare and stammered, "Well I...uhm...d-d-don't plan on it."

"So why did you even bring it up?" Abe countered.

Kiera sighed nervously. She looked at Abe desperately, "I just really want this. You're the only person in the position to help me out like this. Hell, David suggested I ask you."

"But I'm sure David didn't advise you to add that other bullshit in when you asked," Abe said heatedly.

"No," Kiera said quietly. "He didn't."

"Leverage?"

"Something like that."

Abe intertwined his hands and leaned forward. To avoid his stare, Kiera focused on the blinding diamond pinky ring on his right hand.

"Look at me," Abe ordered in a calm but malevolent tone.

Kiera's eyes moved slowly to meet his. Why did she always feel a need to try this man? Kiera was now ready to exit the room as fast as possible. Abe was so unpredictable, and he wore many faces. Kiera was unsure of the face she would get now.

"You let this be the last time you let something stupid come out of your mouth when you talk to me. Do you understand Kiera?"

Kiera nodded.

"You lucky you're David's niece and my brother's baby mama—"

"But your brother isn't the twins—" Kiera was saying until the look Abe gave her silenced her.

"Didn't I just tell you not to let stupid shit come out of your mouth?"

"But—"

"But nothing!"

Kiera looked down at her hands to avoid Abe's angry stare.

"Now, what did you come in here to ask me?" Abe asked in a kinder tone.

Kiera was unsure if she should answer him. She carefully spoke in a timid tone, "I was wondering if you could help me out with my own salon."

There was a dramatic pause before Abe replied, "Sure."

Kiera couldn't contain her excitement. "You will?"

Abe turned his attention back to his computer. "We'll go over the specifics later. But right now; get out of my office Kiera."

Kiera didn't have to be told twice. She quickly got up and headed for the door. Before leaving out of the office, she looked back at Abe and offered him a gracious smile, "Thanks."

Abe dismissed her with a listless wave.

———

Ike couldn't stand the sight of Reggie kissing up to Melissa in front of him. Melissa knew Ike was merely ten feet away, yet she showed no consideration for how Ike might feel. Reggie didn't love Melissa. Didn't she know that? Ike wondered how Melissa would feel if he told her about Reggie's infidelities. He wondered how she would especially feel when she learned that one of Reggie's other women was Ike's very own ex-wife, Tomiko.

Jackie walked over to Ike looking up at him. Damn, he was a tall piece of work. Ike had to be about six feet and six inches tall. "You know you're real obvious. You don't hide your feelings well."

Ike smiled down at Jackie. "Am I obvious?"

"I see it all over your face," Jackie chuckled. "You betta cool it 'fore he come over here and cuss you out about his woman."

Ike looked around the office and whispered to Jackie. "Do you not understand whose place of business this is? That nigga won't do shit. Not with Abe nearby."

Jackie glanced toward Melissa speaking with her husband. "So, are they working things out?"

Ike shrugged. "It looks that way."

"Are you gonna tell her the truth?"

"Not at this time. She ain't ready for the truth."

"C'mon Ike. I would want somebody to tell me the truth," Jackie said.

"And you'd probably cope differently. Melissa is in denial. I really ain't got time for it."

Jackie smiled sneakily as she said, "What do you got time for?"

Ike returned the same sneaky playful smile. "You."

Jackie started laughing and shaking her head. "Naw! Don't even go there."

"You went there first," Ike said in his defense.

Eli was walking by and said, "Y'all sure are chummy."

Ike called after Eli, "Hey! You stay over there."

Jackie caught Melissa glancing over at them wearing a displeased frown. Jackie wasn't trying to step on anybody's toes, but Melissa was snoozing on Ike. If Melissa didn't want Ike, Jackie would gladly take him.

"So, what's up with you and Tomiko anyway?" Jackie asked.

"I'm just about ready to serve those papers. My lawyer getting them ready now," he said.

Jackie nodded her head in thought. "So, you'll be a free man pretty soon."

"Yep. Free to do what the fuck I please."

Jackie's eyes went to Melissa escorting her husband out the front entrance. "What about her?"

"Didn't I just say she confused?"

"Those weren't your words."

"Same shit," he mumbled.

Melissa approached the two of them. She asked Ike, "Can I have a word with you in private please?"

"Sure," Ike said. He looked at Jackie and smiled. "I'll be back. Don't leave without seeing me first."

Jackie nodded, "Okay." She watched Ike join Melissa. His swag was so cool. He always walked as if his dick was too big. The three Masters brothers all walked like that. It was sexy as hell to Jackie.

———

Melissa pulled away from Ike's hold. They had just shared a fervent kiss that awakened everything inside of Melissa. She said, "I can't do this with you, Ike."

85

"Why not?" he asked pleading with his eyes. "I'm this close to filing my divorce with Tomiko. You do yours, and we can be together. You don't have to worry about anything. I got us covered."

"My finances are not what I'm concerned about," Melissa said. "It's the emotional part about all of this."

"I got that covered too," Ike said. "Once we get them out of the way it can only get better for the both of us."

"I don't know," Melissa said. She sighed brushing past him. She sat down in one of the leather chairs on the other side of his desk.

"There you go with that 'I don't know' shit," Ike snipped.

"Well, I don't know!" Melissa said in exasperation. She narrowed her eyes at Ike. "What's up with you and Jackie? Why have y'all all of a sudden gotten so close?"

Ike shrugged. "It's just something that happened. She's cool."

"You like her, don't you?"

"She's okay," Ike said. He stood in front of Melissa and looked down at her. He cupped her face in his hand lovingly, "She ain't you though."

Melissa blushed pushing his hand away. "Stop that."

"It's the truth," he said returning his hand back to her face. "I miss you so much. I need to be with you. When can we see each other again?"

"We're seeing each other now," Melissa answered. She smiled up at him.

"Let's christen my office right now."

"Ike," Melissa said in a stern scolding tone. "I'm not gonna do that with you here."

"So, when can we be together again?" Ike asked.

"I don't know," she said.

Disappointed, Ike mumbled, "Okay Melissa; I gotta work."

Melissa was about to say something but was interrupted when the door pushed open. It was Jackie.

"Hey Ike, I'm about to go now. Lovely needs me," Jackie said.

Ike smiled, but it faded when he looked over at Melissa. He said, "You can go now."

Melissa cut her eyes at him. "You're an ass."

Jackie stepped aside to let Melissa walk by. Before Melissa exited, she threw a glaring dagger towards Jackie. Melissa knew what was going on, but she wasn't about to let it bother her. Ike was the one that wanted to be a part of Mekhi's life, and Melissa would always dangle that before him.

————

Robin sat at the rec room bar pretending to be engrossed by her phone. She was sneaking peeks at Abe and Lovely on the sofa. Lovely was lazily sprawled across Abe's lap looking up into his face. He said something to her that caused Lovely to burst into her usual goofy laughter. Lovely began poking him in his sides. A smile spread across Robin's face as she focused in on Abe as he tried not to laugh and throw Lovely from his lap.

Robin wondered what it felt like to be Lovely in that moment. To be laying there in Abe's lap. She wondered how it felt to be held by his muscular arms. What would it feel like to share the same bed with him? Or to be kissed by him as he was kissing Lovely now. Robin watched as his hand began to rub Lovely's small protruding belly in a loving manner. Why did Abe have to fall for Lovely?

As if he felt Robin watching him, Abe looked up and locked gazes with Robin. He frowned making the moment awkward for Robin. She looked away with embarrassment.

"Why were you staring at them anyway?"

Robin's head jerked in the direction of the voice. An expression of disdain immediately crossed Robin's face. "Why are you even here?"

Kiera took a seat beside Robin at the bar. "To get Bria. She's here with Grace."

Robin rolled her eyes. "Get her and be gone."

"If I remember correctly, this is Lovely's and Abe's house—"

"Lovely's house," Robin corrected.

"Didn't they get married?" Kiera retorted snidely.

"Something like that."

Kiera eyed Robin with suspicion. "I know you ain't jealous."

"Jealous? Lovely's my best friend. Why would I be jealous?" Robin said haughtily.

"Cause bitches like you are the jealous type. Want what your friend has. Is that the case Robin?" Kiera taunted with a teasing smirk. "You want Abe?"

Acting as if she was offended, Robin said, "You're ridiculous, you know that?"

"Not as much as you for wanting to be Lovely," Kiera teased.

"Whatever," Robin mumbled hopping down from the barstool. She was relieved to see Eli coming down the stairs. "Are you ready?"

"Yeah...I was just coming down here to get you," Eli said. "Let me tell my brother bye."

Robin shot Kiera a look to kill. Kiera was wearing a devious grin as she eyed Eli as he walked towards Abe and Lovely. Kiera looked back at Robin and laughed wickedly.

As Eli passed Kiera heading back to Robin, he asked, "What the hell is wrong with you?"

"Keep your eye on that bitch," Kiera said in reference to Robin.

"What?" Eli asked with confusion.

Robin blew air in frustration. "C'mon Eli. Let's just get outta here." She started up the stairs with Eli right behind her.

"Eli!" Kiera called.

"What!"

"You heard what I said."

Eli looked at Robin and asked, "What is she talking about?"

"Who knows? You know she's messy. You said so yourself," Robin said continuing up the stairs. Robin had a sudden feeling that Kiera was going to be a problem. It was like she lived to annoy people on purpose. If Robin had her way, Kiera would be out of the picture. And if Kiera crossed her the wrong way, Robin didn't have a problem with making that happen.

Chapter Six

Time continued to move forward; everyone's lives oblivious to what was brewing in the pot of secrets except the one living in the secret itself.

Seven months later, Abe found himself being the happiest he had ever been in his life. Things were going very well for him. He had a beautiful pregnant wife, a wonderful daughter, business couldn't be better, money was no issue, and his health was top notch. He felt like a new man with a chance of experiencing true happiness. A happiness he didn't want to lose.

Lovely was lying on her side in bed when Abe entered their bedroom. He got in bed behind her. "*Te amo mi amor,*" he whispered in her ear.

Lovely wrapped his arm around her. Abe rubbed her stomach.

"He must be asleep."

"He'll be up flip-flopping in a couple of hours," Lovely mumbled.

Abe kissed Lovely's neck softly. His hand traveled to her full breasts and massaged them. Lovely moaned. *Her hot ass,* Abe thought. He brought his hand back down to rub her through her panties. "Can I have this?"

Lovely chided playfully, "Spanish. You know better."

Abe smiled, "*¿Puedo tener esto?*"

"*Sí, mi gran amante fuerte,*" Lovely replied.

Abe giggled, "You're crazy. Big strong lover? Seriously?"

Lovely giggled too. She removed her panties.

Abe removed his bottoms as he said, "Lovely, you're nine months pregnant and still wanna fuck every night."

"Not every night," she said reaching back to stroke him. He was aroused. "He ain't got a problem with it."

"He never does," he said kissing her gently on her neck as he worked himself deep within Lovely's walls.

Lovely breathed, "Oh my...God." She held onto the bed tightly as he stroked her from behind. Lovely met his stroke with her own thrusts. She could never get enough of him. She threw it back on him harder than he was giving.

Abe fussed, "Slow your ass down before you hurt the baby."

"We can't hurt him," she said.

Abe bit her neck gently whispering, "*Eres una chica mala.*"

Lovely smiled. She placed his hand in between her legs. He began rubbing her clit as he continued to stroke her at an even pace. Lovely was stimulated into an addictive orgasm. Her body tensed up causing her to pull a round ligament on the side she laid on. "Ow...shit!"

"What? I hurt you? I quit," Abe said rapidly.

"No. I'm fine...Finish," Lovely said. She patted his arm. "Come on."

Abe finished making love to her but at a gentler pace. Although he could have continued he stopped when she was satisfied.

At about two in the morning, Lovely was awakened by an intense contraction that came out of nowhere. She had been feeling them off and on, but this was the real thing. Before she could wake Abe, she was having another one.

"Abe," Lovely said softly. He didn't respond. She sat up. Another contraction hit. This time she cried out in pain and smacked Abe at the same time.

Abe instantly awakened. "What the fuck!"

"It's time, but I don't think...," she was saying. She clutched handfuls of the sheets as another contraction came.

Still, in a groggy stupor, Abe stared at Lovely while his brain tried to register what was happening. Looking at the pained face Lovely was making, it quickly dawned on him that Lovely was in labor. "Oh shit!"

Abe hopped out of bed and got dressed. He went around the bed to her side to help her out of the bed. Lovely stood but didn't move as she shook her head frantically, "I can't!"

"Yes, you can," Abe said.

"No, I can't!" she cried before she started wailing. Her water broke and began trickling down her legs.

Abe observed the liquid trickle down her legs and form puddles at her feet. "Does this mean we won't have time to get to the hospital?"

"Get me a towel so I—Oooh!" she doubled over in pain. Once the contraction passed, she ordered Abe to get her a towel, shoes, and Aunt Livy.

Minutes later Abe was driving Lovely to the hospital with not only Aunt Livy who was coaching Lovely through the contractions, but Grace had awakened and had to tag along. When they told Lulu what was going on, she insisted on going too.

By the time Eli and Robin made it to the hospital, Lovely had already given birth to a seven-pound four-ounce baby boy. He was born with a head full of jet black silky fine hair that hugged to his small round head. His skin was extremely fair. They told Lovely he had dark grey eyes.

"So, he doesn't look nothing like me?" Lovely asked.

"Nope," Eli said. "He looks just like his daddy."

"Yeah, Abe spit him out," Aunt Livy said hovering over the baby's clear bassinet.

Abe sat beside Lovely on her bed. He was proud. He had his first child, a son who would be named after him. Just watching AJ and admiring his little fingers, his tiny shapely lips, button nose, and his curious eyes warmed Abe's heart. He had to blink back tears several times although he actually cried with Lovely when she gave her last push that brought AJ into this world. Words couldn't describe the joy Abe was feeling inside.

Abe kissed the top of Lovely's head. "You did good baby."

————

Kiera got to the fifth floor and found her way to Lovely's room which was already filled with every floral arrangement, stuffed animal, balloons, and gift baskets every gift shop in Nashville had.

"Dang, it's just been two hours," Kiera exclaimed. "Where all this stuff come from?"

Eli pointed to his older brother, "He had to buy one of everything for the baby on top of the stuff he got for Lovely."

Abe defended himself, "I didn't get all of this...just half of it."

Kiera went straight for the glass bassinet holding the Masters, Baby boy. He was so tiny. Kiera's heart swelled with adoration for how pretty the boy was. He was very content. Kiera lifted the cap on his head. A blanket of silky, shiny black hair laid flat to his head. At her touch, his eyes opened. Kiera gasped with surprise, "Oh my God! He looks just like Abe."

Lovely frowned playfully, "So I heard."

"I want another baby now," Kiera said.

Lovely grinned towards Abe, "Did we start something baby?"

Abe said, "I think we did."

Kiera turned away glancing at Eli and Robin in the process. She went to the sink and washed her hands. She wondered about the seriousness of Eli's and Robin's relationship. She heard they had been seeing each other off and on, but it hadn't been stable. She wondered what was going on there. Even more, she wondered if she still had a chance with Eli.

Kiera picked up the baby whose eyes had opened. She sat down beside Eli on the built-in bench seating. "Is he hungry?"

Eli watched Kiera handle the baby in such a delicate way. She seemed so nurturing, so loving, so caring. He wondered if she had been like that with the twins. That thought made him wonder about the paternity of the twins again. Eli was convinced that they were his kids. However, that was an issue that Eli hadn't bothered with since Kiera insisted that they had a father.

Abe noticed the sullen look on Eli's face. "Eli? You okay?"

Eli's eyes cut to Abe. He nodded, "I'm fine. Why you ask?"

"I don't know...you look kinda bothered. You sure you're okay?" Abe asked again.

"I'm fine," Eli repeated. Changing the subject, Eli said, "I wonder if Mama will sneak her ass up here."

There was a knock on the already ajar door. Lovely said cheerfully, "Come in."

Abe who was sitting on the edge of Lovely's bed beside her admired the glow of Lovely's face. She was indeed lovely although she had just given birth about five hours earlier. Her shiny black hair was brushed up into a neat bun atop her head. Her eyes sparkled. Her face was radiant even though it was fuller. Abe wanted to love Lovely forever.

"Wow! Someone is very special."

Luciano's low smooth voice laced with a light Italian accent made Lovely's eyes widen with glee. She exclaimed, "Luciano!"

Abe turned around to look at Lovely's godfather and her grandfather's old friend and business partner. Luciano wore a grey suit with a crisp white button-down shirt, albeit a tie. He was a tall, slender man. He wore his black hair that was streaked with gray cut low with white hair at his temples. He wore a very distinguished neatly trimmed white goatee and beard that matched his hair. His eyes were the same sterling blue, almost grey that contrasted with his olive skin as Abe's did with his golden honey complexion. There was almost an uncanny resemblance between Abe and the older man that Abe still found odd.

First things first, Luciano greeted Lovely with a peck to either cheek. "You look swell *mio tesoro*."

"I'm so glad you came," Lovely grinned. "It seems like Abe just talked to you."

Luciano looked at Abe and smiled, "Abe. Didn't I tell you Lovely would be giving birth before the week was out?"

Abe reluctantly nodded. "Yeah, you told me."

"What? Y'all had a bet?" Eli asked.

"Lu is always betting on something," Abe said. He and Luciano had grown closer as friends and as business associates. Abe had been elated that Luciano was pleased with his presentation of the designs for the resort. Luciano commented on how thorough and professional Abe kept things. Most of the time compliments from his clients rarely stroked his ego and confidence but hearing praises from Luciano meant something to Abe. He had a lot of respect for the older gentleman. Looking at Luciano, Abe could only hope that he was in the same physical health thirty years from now.

Luciano stood over Kiera admiring the baby. "He's gonna be a handsome fella."

"Yeah, like his daddy," Abe beamed.

"Where's Cesar?" Lovely asked.

"Cesar is in Italy," Luciano answered absently. He asked, "Does the baby have Abe's eyes?"

"They're a greyish color," Kiera answered.

Luciano let out an amused chuckled. Luciano was proud as he smiled down at his grandchild.

An hour later, the nurses came back for the baby for additional testing. Abe decided that visitation was over and insisted that his wife needed to rest, so he put everyone out.

Luciano was the last to leave. He asked Abe, "So, how does it feel to have a little copy of yourself?"

"It's a great feeling," Abe answered.

"Indeed, it is," Luciano said with a smile. He looked at Abe long and wanted badly to let him know that he was his father. It wasn't the right time though; however, Luciano had every intention on telling Abe the truth whether Sarah was okay with it or not.

Chapter Seven

Kiera had been on her feet doing hair for twelve hours. She really didn't feel like going to the grocery store, but Vanessa asked if she could pick some items up for her. Kiera felt like it was the least she could do since Vanessa had been very helpful in caring for the twins.

Before heading to the checkout, Kiera remembered she needed some personal hygiene products.

A familiar voice deterred her from what she set out to do. Kiera knew she heard his voice before she could see him. She could recognize the raspiness, roughness of Lorenzo's voice anywhere. He was loud and obnoxious as he was known for being. Who walks around the store talking that loud on the phone?

Lorenzo was the nephew of Esau Masters which made him Abe and Eli's cousin. Back in the day, Lorenzo otherwise known as Loco ran wild in the streets. He ran in Abe's circle of hoodlums under Antino Mancuso's direction. Lorenzo was crazy. If Antino needed a message sent by way of torture it was Loco that he used. He was into beating and raping women. He would hit and kill a kid. It didn't matter to him. If a person jumped stupid his way, he wouldn't let down until the person got the picture that they had messed up when they decided to fuck with him.

"Boy will you shut up! All that damn loud ass talking," Kiera yelled at Lorenzo's back.

"Who the hell...Ay hold on real quick," he said as he turned around ready to break the person's neck that yelled at him.

Kiera stood there grinning. When he realized who she was, he softened and smiled. He said into the phone, "Ay, let me call you back my nigga."

"Yeah, that's what I thought," Kiera smirked.

"What's up girl," he crooned immediately wrapping his arms around her in a warm hug.

Kiera returned the warmth. "Nothing. I thought that was you being all loud and shit."

"Fuck that shit," he said standing back to take in the sight of her wholly. "You looking good."

Kiera looked at him. Lorenzo, despite his craziness, was a good-looking dude. He had a little Dominican in him like his uncle, Esau. He was tall like Abe, but he didn't have the same clean, pretty looks as Abe and Eli. Lorenzo had a ruggedness that he acquired in the streets. He was thick like Abe but not cut up like Abe although he was pretty solid.

Kiera asked, "Whatchu been up to?"

"You know I just got out of prison girl. I did seven years."

"Really? I didn't know that. I was wondering where you were missing all of the action."

"What'cho ass talking 'bout?"

"You know I just returned to Nashville some months ago."

"That's good but what action you talking 'bout?"

Kiera grinned. Still being evasive she said, "When the last time you had contact with Big Ant?"

"I'm on my way to see his ass now. We got business to discuss."

"You don't fuck with your cousin no more?" Kiera asked.

"Who?"

"Abe."

Lorenzo grunted falling into thought. "Ol Abe. So, what's he been up to lately? I thought he was all good boy now. Can't help a nigga out and shit."

"Abe is good people. He let me stay with him when I first got here. Now I have my own place. He put me in one of his properties."

"Oh yeah."

"Yeah. You oughta give him a call."

"I might just do that."

There was something sinister about the way he was looking that didn't settle right with Kiera. She went on through the line to pay for her items and noticed that Lorenzo was following behind her.

"You get what you came in here for?" Kiera asked looking at his empty hands.

"Naw but it can wait now," he said. "C'mon let's go talk."

Kiera followed Lorenzo out to his vehicle which was a brand-new black on black Tahoe. Something told Kiera his seeing Antino today wouldn't be the first time he had seen him since being released from prison.

"So, tell me about Abe. That nigga still got a lot of money?"

"You know he do. Don't your uncle keep you informed?"

"He know only what Auntie Sarah wants him to know. But I heard Abe was doing the damn thing."

"Well, he got a wife now. He seems to be really happy with her."

"Oh yeah."

"Yeah," she said. Then the thought hit her. "Oh yeah! You know who his wife is?"

"Who?"

"Remember that Indian dude that used to own that corner store across from the projects out North?"

Lorenzo gave it some thought. How could he forget Pras? A smile came to his face as he remembered. "Yeah."

"She's dude's daughter."

"What?" Lorenzo asked in shock.

"Yeah. I remembered her," Kiera said with a nod.

"Are you for real?" Lorenzo asked. He had to be hearing Kiera incorrectly.

"Yeah. I'm positive. Isn't it a small world?"

"It sho in the fuck is," Lorenzo said under his breath as he gave the situation some deep thought.

Kiera said, "You know what's weird? She's legally blind now. I don't really know the full story, but I remember all that shit that went down with y'all."

"Oh yeah," Lorenzo said entertaining the thought. He spoke his thought aloud, "I wonder...does Abe know who she is?"

"He does now."

A wicked grin spread across Lorenzo's face.

"What?" Kiera asked.

Lorenzo just shook his head. "So whatchu finna get into?" he asked her.

As Kiera was about to answer she looked up and saw a familiar face smiling in her direction. The woman waved at her and started making her way over. "Kiera! I thought that was you!"

"Oh shit," Kiera hissed.

Lorenzo eyed the female taking in as much of her svelte frame as he could. "Who is that?"

Kiera rolled her eyes, "Somebody really annoying."

Aisha wore a huge smile as she came to stand before them. "Hey girl!"

Why is she talking to me like we're cool, Kiera thought? One of the stylists that rented a booth at Shear Elegance happened to be Aisha's hairstylists. Whenever Aisha came into the salon, she would carry on as if she and Kiera were the best of friends. Kiera knew Aisha simply wanted to keep up with what Abe was doing through her.

Aisha looked up at Lorenzo flashing him a seductive smile. "Kiera, I thought you were over here talking to Abe."

Kiera let out a sarcastic laugh. Lorenzo may have been just as tall as Abe, but there was no way a person could mistake the two. "Really Aisha? Why would I be talking to Abe in the heat in the middle of the grocery store parking lot?"

Aisha shrugged. She looked at Lorenzo and asked, "So who are you?"

"I'm Lorenzo," he replied enjoying the presence of the blond-haired beauty before him. Her green eyes reminded him of round cut peridot gems.

Lorenzo nudged Kiera. "Damn girl, you ain't gon introduce us."

"It seem like y'all were handling that fine on your own," Kiera said. "But if you must know, this is Aisha. She's actually Abe's ex."

"You used to go with Abe?" Lorenzo said looking Aisha up and down.

Aisha rolled her eyes, "Yeah that was the past. Abe is a married man now...so fuck him."

"Yeah, fuck that nigga," Lorenzo repeated with a slight laugh.

Kiera looked at the two of them in disbelief. "Are y'all serious right now?"

"What?" Aisha asked innocently.

"You looking at Abe's cousin like you wanna jump his damn bones," Kiera stated.

Aisha gave a slight shrug with a raised eyebrow as if she was giving it some thought.

Kiera shook her head. "Well, I'm finna go and leave you two to yourselves. Lo, I'll see you around. And Aisha, I guess I'll see you when you come in the shop to get that weave tighten."

Aisha gave Kiera her middle finger.

Kiera laughed. She turned to Lorenzo and asked incredulously, "You'd holla at her after Abe?"

He replied arrogantly, "It ain't like we never did that shit before."

———

Sarah was getting herself dressed for an evening with her in-laws. She didn't prefer to hang out with the Masters. They were all rogues and lowlifes. The Masters surname sound dignitary and stately but the only thing stately about the family was a Tennessee State Prison. Shit. Her boys were the only things that brought some honor to the name.

Sarah asked Esau, "How long will we be at your brother's house?"

"You got somewhere else to be?" Esau asked smartly.

"Well," she sighed clasping her three-carat tennis bracelet on her wrist. "I was wanting to visit the boys."

"Where?"

"At Abe's," she answered flatly while looking at him blankly.

"Abe's?" Esau asked in disbelief.

"Yes, Abe. You know, my son."

"Oh. He's your son now?"

Sarah got up from her vanity to enter her boudoir. "He's always been, my son."

"Really?" he asked with amusement as he stood behind her.

Sarah looked back at him and cut her eyes. She slipped on her Jimmy Choo slingbacks. She walked past Esau with an air of arrogance. "You know Esau, all of this crazy animosity is tiresome. It's time I made amends with my son."

"How long have you been thinking this?" Esau asked following Sarah out of the bedroom.

"A while now," Sarah said. She looked at him knowingly.

"Are you sure this ain't got nothing to do with Lu and that girl?"

Sarah saw the malice dancing in his eyes. She wished she hadn't revealed to Esau that Luciano de Rosa was Abe's wife's godfather. If Esau got any ideas, Sarah would be the blame for this on top of the already long list of wrongdoings she asked God to forgive her on. "It has nothing to do with them either."

"Well, it just seem odd that when they enter the picture, you wanna be active in Abe's life."

"Abe has had my first grandchild. I don't wanna miss out on all of the baby's precious moments."

Esau rolled his eyes upwards shaking his head in disbelief. "You're something else, Sarah."

"I kinda like Lovely," Sarah said as an afterthought.

Esau frowned. "Lovely?"

Sarah nodded. "Yeah. That's her name. You know that. Stop acting dumb Esau."

"I didn't know what her name was. You always refer to her as that girl that married Abe."

"I've mentioned her name before."

"No, you have not," Esau insisted.

"Whatever. Let's go," she said flippantly.

The usual drunks, weed heads, thugs, sluts, and crumb snatching delinquents were at Bobby's disguised as middle-class citizens in a nice neighborhood of Northridge. They were hood rich and still lived within a hood mentality.

"Hey, Sarah!" Valencia greeted cheerfully.

Sarah gave her sister-in-law a hug only because it was the polite thing to do. The den was cluttered with gossiping women. Most of the men were in the basement.

Valencia said, "Have a seat."

Sarah sat at the dinette table separating the kitchen from the den.

"Where the boys?" Mama Dot asked.

"You know where they at," Reese sneered. Reese was Esau's sister who had a publicized disdain for Sarah's children. "You know *they* too good for us."

No, Sarah thought, *it's just y'all have always mistreated them. And I let y'all; shame on me.*

"You know I ran into Eli the other day," Valencia said. "He had some kids and a woman with him at the store. He married too?"

"No," Sarah shook her head.

"Whose kids were those?" Valencia asked.

"They Abe's kids?" Mama Dot asked.

Sarah shook her head. "Abe's wife's daughter and her friend."

"What's up Auntie!"

The hairs on the back of Sarah's neck stood up. The sound of his voice froze Sarah with dread. Aw hell, she thought.

Lorenzo "Loco" Harris son of Reese. The biggest menace to society there was. He used to run the streets as a juvenile. Rumor has it he hooked up with Abe and his violent gang of degenerates. Lorenzo was dumb and hot-headed.

There was a fallen out after Lorenzo got busted by the feds. All of his belongings and the little empire he was building were all confiscated. At that time Abe had already walked away from the streets. Lorenzo and the others that fell to their demise expected Abe to step in and replenish their drug operations. Abe couldn't and wouldn't do it.

So, while Sarah was enjoying the riches, Abe bestowed on her Reese had to return to public housing, a job as a high school cafeteria worker, and drive a 2001 Chevrolet Lumina. Sarah chuckled to herself just thinking about it.

Sarah asked, "When you get out?" Lorenzo gave her a hug. Sarah looked to make sure her jewels were still on. His ass was a good thief.

"Shiid...I been out," Lorenzo said eyeing Sarah's attire and accessories. "I heard Abe doing the damn thang."

Sarah nodded suddenly feeling uncomfortable. Lorenzo spent about seven years in prison. He was bigger, more muscular. He had acquired several tattoos which made his once fair skin look like he rubbed himself with cigarette ashes. His fine curly hair was cut in a low curly afro. That was the only good thing about the Masters; their mixed heritage made them fairly attractive people.

"My brother finna come through and we heading over Abe's house in a minute," Lorenzo told Sarah.

"You are? Abe know you out?" Sarah asked.

"I guess he do," Lorenzo said nonchalantly.

Sarah said, "Loco, you know Abe don't get down like that no more."

Lorenzo chuckled. "I know Auntie. I just need to holla at him." He gestured to Sarah to follow him down the hall for privacy.

Sarah was reluctant to do it, but she needed to know what this boy had up his sleeve.

"You tell your people about that lick we made for Antino?" he asked.

"Why would I and risk getting Abe in trouble or killed? Like I told you then when you were running your mouth, and I found out who y'all hit you fucked with the wrong family. Leave well enough alone. Leave Abe alone. Nashville has been at peace. We don't need no mafia wars going on."

"You know something don't you," Lorenzo said with suspicion. He eyed Sarah's bracelet. "Give me that."

"No," she said defiantly.

"Abe give it to you?"

"Don't worry about it. You're not getting it." Sarah walked away with an air of assurance and confidence, but she was trembling with fear on the inside. She didn't even bother saying bye to anyone or telling Esau she was leaving. She jumped in Esau's new BMW X5 that Abe gave him for his birthday and peeled off.

———

Sarah stared back into the icy grey cold eyes of Antino. "What are you up to?"

"I have no idea what you're talking about?" Antino said smugly in his smooth voice.

Antino was the more handsome between him and Luciano, although they looked a lot alike. After all, they were brothers. Sarah had always wanted to be with Antino, but he was too obnoxious and arrogant for any woman to stand him for too long. After numerous advances, Sarah had given in to Antino years ago. He had been hard to resist. When she discovered she was pregnant with Abe, she tried going to Antino about it. He brushed her off like she was some ordinary woman in the streets. Fearing that he would tell Luciano and it get back to Esau, Sarah decided to go with the rape story just in case her child was not Esau's. It was easy to pass Eli off as Esau child, but the truth of the matter was Sarah was unsure about both Ike's and Eli's paternity as well. It could have been any one of the three. Esau never questioned her about Ike's or Eli's paternity but when he saw Abe's blue eyes he knew without a reasonable doubt that Abe was not his child.

Although neither man possess the same blue eyes as Abe, between Luciano and Antino, one of them was his father.

"Are you putting Lorenzo up to do your dirty work?" Sarah asked.

"Again, I know not what you speak of," he said. He eyed Sarah from her breasts to her thighs. There was no reason to look elsewhere. He said, "You're looking good Sarah."

"I heard you don't like 'em as old as me," she smirked.

"I don't," he said arrogantly.

Sarah rolled her eyes. She asked, "When was the last time you heard from your brother?"

"Just the other day. He's doing well. I'll let him know you asked about him. What's the reason for your visit Sarah?" he asked a bit annoyed.

"Do you know Lovely is alive?" she questioned with a raised brow.

"Yes, I do."

"What are your plans?"

"Why would I tell you that?"

"Okay. Just know that Abe is involved with her."

"Sarah, I'm not thinking of Lovely," he said. Then he laughed heartily. "Although it would be a shame for her to find out that the people surrounding her are a bunch of liars. How do you think she would feel about that?"

"What do you want?"

He gave it some thought. "Absolutely nothing."

Sarah narrowed her eyes. "Leave Abe be. Don't involve him in none of your dirty work Antino."

Antino pierced Sarah with his gaze. "You're talking to the wrong person."

Sarah exhaled heavily. She asked, "Now what are you talking about?"

"I have no ill feelings toward Abe," he answered. "He was and always will be like a son to me."

Sarah let out a laugh laced with sarcasm. "Yeah right. Abe wouldn't want anything to do with you."

"How would you know that Sarah?"

"Because he's above the vile things you're involved in."

"Vile? My life very much mimics Abe's life. We're like one in the same."

"Hardly. Abe is the pillar of the community."

Antino scoffed in amusement. This woman was a piece of work. Getting off the subject Antino said, "Lorenzo should not be a worry of Abe's. I will make sure of it. I'll have a talk with him."

Sarah turned away making the sleeves of her caftan dress sway. "A talk? I know how cunning you can be. Abe hasn't been this happy in a while. Leave him be."

"Happy? How would you know? You talk to him now?"

Sarah stopped in the middle of the foyer before reaching his front door. "Me and my son are just fine."

"Sure, you are," he said going to the door. "Don't forget Sarah who you're speaking to. I know everything."

Sarah cut her eyes as he let her out. There was no way Antino or Luciano would mess this up for her.

Chapter Eight

Lorenzo was not Aisha's type. He was thuggish and street. He was a far cry from his cousin Abe. Abe was so polished and corporate casual. He knew how to speak like the intelligent man he was although around those closest to him he became very informal. She used to love that about Abe. He had so many faces. Being with him was soothing and never dull. However, Lorenzo was fine, and he was Abe's relative. What would be the most hurtful spiteful thing Aisha could do to get under Abe's skin?

Truth be told, Aisha was definitely feeling salty about Abe's new life with his wife and newborn. She kept up with his life through Kiera. It had Aisha feeling some type of way. She now had a mission to get Abe back or at least make him unhappy. In her delusional mind, if she couldn't be the one he was with, then he couldn't be happy with someone else.

A text came through on her phone. She immediately smiled when she saw who it was. It read: *wyd*?

She replied: *nothing...what's up?*

Can u talk?

Aisha placed the call. Lorenzo answered, "What's up beautiful?"

"I see I be on somebody's mind all the time."

"You already know. So, what's up wit' ya?"

"Just sitting here all by myself," she said in her sweetest softest voice.

"Oh yeah. You need some company?"

Aisha smiled as if Lorenzo could see her. She said, "You trying to get with your cousin's ex?"

"I ain't looking at you as Abe's ex. To me you another beautiful woman who I'd like to get to know. Ya feel me?"

"Oh, I definitely feel you."

———

About a week after that little meeting in the parking lot, Kiera found herself in Aisha's company again. Kiera couldn't believe she was actually in the car with Aisha. Since Aisha's stylist was busy and Kiera was not, Kiera volunteered to show Aisha where she could buy a particular brand of hair for a reasonable price. Kiera wished she had kept her mouth shut. Riding around Nashville with Aisha was annoying and aggravating. To top it off, she couldn't drive worth a damn!

Aisha grinned at Kiera as he she hopped in her car. "C'mon tramp. You're so slow."

Kiera put her seatbelt on. "I wasn't that slow. You're the one that take all day."

"Yeah, but I gotta get over to Lorenzo's real quick."

Kiera gave Aisha side eye. "I don't wanna go over there. Take me back to my shop. So, you and Lorenzo are really serious huh?"

Aisha smiled as thoughts of Lorenzo crossed her mind. "Yeah, something like that."

"You're trifling," Kiera said shaking her head with a slight laugh.

"Not any more trifling than you are. You don't even know who your kids' father is?" Aisha countered.

"Yeah, whatever," Kiera said dismissively. The thought of her twins' father made her cringe. She wished Eli was their father for real because Kiera would much rather deal with Eli than him. He never wanted to see them, and he barely supplied her with support. She didn't need her twins' father anymore anyway. Abe had come through for her like he said he would. Her salon Shear Elegance had been up and running for three months, and business was looking good.

"You don't mind me stopping by Lorenzo's real quick right?" Aisha asked again.

Kiera groaned, "I'm really not trying to be around him like that."

Aisha gave Kiera a sneaky smile. "Lorenzo's brother might be over here."

Kiera rolled her eyes hard. "Who the fuck cares?"

"Ain't y'all fucking? Lorenzo told me you and his brother had a thing."

"Naw! That nasty nigga can't touch me. You screwing Lorenzo?" Kiera asked.

Aisha snickered. "Something like that."

Kiera asked out of curiosity, "So tell me something, Aisha. Sex...Lo or Abe?"

Aisha gave it some thought as she tried to focus on the road. "If I answer that honestly..."

"What other way is there to answer it?" Kiera interjected. "It's just us. You can be honest with me."

Aisha said, "Abe could fuck the shit out of a bitch. And his head was even better."

Kiera grinned. "So, Abe it is."

"Hell yeah. But Lo can put it down too."

"Do you miss being with Abe?"

Aisha smiled, "Of course I do. But I enjoy the wildness of being with Lo."

"You just want a bad boy."

"I do. But I do miss me some Abe," Aisha grinned as thoughts of the past swirled in her mind.

Kiera grinned sly, "You know Abe used to be worse than Lo. He was an ultimate bad boy."

"He was?"

"He turned over a new leaf on life," Kiera said with thought as she gazed out of the window. "I think it's time I do so too."

"Don't tell me you're about to get all good girl on me?" Aisha teased.

"I'm just tired. And I want a good man in my life."

"Well it certainly ain't Eli," Aisha said. "He don't want you. You're a girl."

Kiera said, "I don't think Eli is gay."

"That's bullshit. He's gay. Why hasn't he ever had a girlfriend? I've never seen Eli with a girl," Aisha said matter of factly.

Kiera wouldn't argue with Aisha on that subject. She started pecking on her phone to send Eli a message. *Hey you*

A minute later Eli replied: *hey*

Kiera: *thinking of you*

No response. Kiera frowned. After ten minutes, Aisha was pulling up to Lorenzo's brother's place, and there was still no response. Kiera text: *did I do something wrong?*

Eli: *yeah...you exist...stop texting me and make that appt*

"Are you getting out?" Aisha asked as she grabbed her purse from the backseat.

Kiera nodded not taking her eyes from her phone as she tapped away. *I swear you get on my nerves*

Aisha opened her door and said, "Oh he said his uncle would probably be here when I got here. Too bad I didn't get to meet him. I wonder if that's his...," her voice trailed as her eyes tried to focus on the woman sitting on the passenger side in the vehicle she was eyeing. The vehicle began to pull off from the curb. "I was gonna say, that looks like...That is her! Kiera, look."

Kiera looked up in time to see Robin sitting on the passenger side of a black BMW X5. What the hell, Kiera thought. She ducked down into her seat to make sure she was out of view. She didn't want Robin to know she had seen her. However, this was very interesting.

———

Hesitant about starting a messy situation, Kiera opted to keep what she recently witnessed to herself. However, she felt it put her at an advantage when it came to Eli. She smiled with a fraction of victory as she rung Eli's gate. It was late, and he probably would have an attitude that she had come by so late.

A minute later the gate opened, and she drove up the driveway. Eager to see him she hurried out of the car. The front door opened to darkness. Eli motioned for her to come inside. She stepped in and asked, "Why is it so dark down here? And how come you didn't ask who it was? I know your intercom works."

"Ain't nobody down here. It's the foyer. And I saw you on the damn monitor. I recognized your big-headed ass. C'mon," he said leading the way upstairs where there was plenty of lighting.

Kiera could see Eli was wearing only black lounge pants. She could see his nice body even in the darkness of the staircase. He led her to his kitchen where he apparently had been because there was a glass of brown liquor on the counter.

"What are you doing awake?" Kiera asked.

"Waiting on people like you to ring my damn doorbell at eleven at night," he joked.

"Whatever. I thought you were an early sleeper."

"Couldn't really sleep."

Kiera watched him go to his refrigerator and just stare inside of it. Kiera said, "What's that in that Chinese takeout container?"

"General Tso's chicken. You want it? It was from earlier today."

"Yeah, lemme get some of that," Kiera said. "I don't know why I'm so damn hungry."

"You ain't pregnant, are you?" Eli asked.

"You gotta be having sex to get pregnant, right?"

Eli laughed. "Are you trying to say your freaky ass ain't been having sex?"

Kiera shook her head, "I'm saving myself for you."

"Sure, you are."

Kiera grinned sneakily. "I am. You'll come to your senses one day."

They talked while they ate. Although things with Kiera had been rocky in the past, Eli was beginning to like her as a person. She wasn't so bad after all.

In the middle of their conversation, Eli's phone rang. He looked at the display. He motioned for Kiera to be quiet. He answered, "Hello?"

"What are you doing?" Robin asked. Her tone was indifferent.

Eli returned the same dry tone, "Nothing."

"I thought you were gonna call me back."

"Well I changed my mind," he said with annoyance.

"So, this is how you wanna act?"

"What do you mean?" Eli asked immediately becoming defensive.

"You've been acting really funny lately Eli," Robin said.

Over the past seven months, Eli has enjoyed his time spent with Robin, but the energy between them had sizzled. On top of that, Robin was becoming clingier. She wanted to be an official couple. Eli wasn't ready to settle down with one woman, and if he did, he wasn't sure if he wanted it to be Robin as he thought before.

"Your silence speaks volumes, Eli," Robin said. "If you don't wanna be in an exclusive relationship with me then it's cool. But understand I'm not going to sit back and wait on you."

"So, what are you gonna do? Run back to the married dude?" Eli asked.

Kiera grabbed her glass of wine and gestured to Eli that she was headed in the den. Eli nodded his acknowledgment as he continued his conversation.

Kiera wondered what Eli would think if he knew the married dude Robin was involved with was someone he knew. Kiera giggled to herself as she began channel surfing.

———

Kiera awakened that morning to her phone chiming. She reached over the sofa's arm feeling for her purse that she knew had to be on the end table.

"Your purse is on the floor," Eli told her.

Kiera sat up fully and turned towards his voice. He was standing in his kitchen in a white t-shirt and plaid pajama bottoms. Kiera just loved his height and slim athletic build.

"You hungry?" he asked.

"Are you cooking?"

He laughed. "Yeah right. I don't cook."

"Man, you better learn. So, what did you have in mind?"

"I'm in the mood for Hardees," he said crossing the den to head to his bedroom.

Kiera's phone chimed again. She answered it. "Hello?"

"Hey Keke," Vanessa said cheerfully.

"Hey. I'll be there to get the twins in just a minute," Kiera quickly said.

"Oh no, you're fine. I was calling to let you know that they're going to church with David and me. So, don't get in no rush."

"Oh...Okay," Kiera said. "How have they been doing? They've been behaving?"

"Yeah. They're no problem."

"Okay. Well, call me when you make it back home."

"Will do sweetie."

Once the call ended Kiera got up and went to Eli's bedroom. He was laying on his back on his bed with the remote in his hand. Kiera said, "I can't believe you let me sleep over here."

"Your ass was knocked out. I got off the phone with Robin, and you were drooling on my couch. Did you even feel when I put the cover on you?"

Kiera shook her head. "It was that wine."

Eli looked at Kiera with thought. He asked, "So are we gonna get this DNA test scheduled."

Kiera rolled her eyes upward. "Here you go."

"C'mon Kee. I need to know that they're not mine. They look just like me. I'm convinced they're mine. Now I haven't bothered you in a long while about this, but every time I see them, I can't help but think those are my children."

Kiera sighed. Although she didn't know for sure, Kiera felt in her heart that Eli was not the twins' father. "Okay. If it'll shut you up and stop you from bugging me about that shit."

"That's all I want."

"So why did you let me stay here? Out of spite?"

Eli frowned up. "Out of spite to who?"

"Robin. Y'all having problems ain't y'all?"

"I ain't thinking about Robin's ass. To be honest, I don't think she into me like that. It's like she's got ulterior motives."

"Why do you say that?" Kiera asked curiously.

"Well, one minute she's getting on my nerves about wanting to be in a committed relationship, and then the next minute she's telling me to do me because she doing her. And she sleeps away from Lovely's house most of the time when she isn't here. She seeing somebody else. So, what the fuck she in my face for?"

"I don't know why you won't swing my way," she said with a sly smile.

"Uhm maybe because you're full of shit too," Eli retorted. He asked, "You still hungry? I am."

"How are you hungry and you got back in bed?"

"Cause I'm really not ready to get up. Go get me some food."

"I ain't fetching shit for you," Kiera laughed. "But I'll be glad to ride along with you."

"Okay. Let me jump in the shower first," Eli said as he sprang from his bed.

"Hey, how big is the damn bed because you're pretty tall and your whole body is swallowed in this mug."

"It's twelve by ten. I had to have a big bed." He added with a wink, "That's my king."

"I see," Kiera said. "Do you mind if I sit in here while you handle your business?"

"Nah, go right ahead. Don't be tryna come in here peeking either," he teased.

Kiera grinned, "Well you don't come out here naked."

Kiera kicked back on the huge bed channel surfing. She settled on an old episode of MTV's Catfish. She heard the shower running. She wondered if she could sneak a peek without him noticing. Her crush for Eli went beyond crush level. Kiera found herself being obsessed but not in a psychotic way.

She went to the bathroom and pushed the door open. Once it opened wide enough, she eased inside the steamy bathroom. He was in the shower, but it was hard to make him out. How would he feel if she got in there with him, she wondered? It wouldn't be the most outrageous thing she had done to Eli. *Go for it Kiera*, she told herself. She quietly undressed and let her clothing drop to the floor. Kiera opened the door to the huge walk-in shower and stepped in.

"What the..." Eli was stunned.

"Ssh, just go with it," Kiera grinned. She took in the sight of him from head to toe. Her eyes lingered a little too long on his long soapy dick. She said, "You look good naked."

Eli looked her up and down too. He said, "So do you."

Without hesitation or a second thought, Kiera reached out and started stroking him lathering the soap up even more. The soap made the stroke smooth and steady. She looked up into Eli's eyes as he stared back at her with wonderment. She was so glad he allowed her to do this which could only mean two things: he was feeling the same way about her, or he just needed a fix because he was frustrated. Either way, Kiera was going to take advantage of it.

Kiera could hear Eli's breathing becoming shallower, and he shuddered beneath her touch. He was about to cum, so she couldn't stop. She stimulated the frenulum and head of his dick to get him there faster. Then out of nowhere, he busted, and it startled Kiera for some reason. Eli wore an amused smile on his face.

"What you smiling about?" she asked as she gently continued stroking him until he was empty.

"You. You won't stop, will you?"

"What do you mean?"

"You're determined to have me...again."

"It's something that I really want."

Eli bent to kiss her softly on the lips. He asked, "Can I have you?"

That single act alone had Kiera excited inside. Kiera caught her bottom lip in between her teeth and nodded. Eli gestured toward the built-in shower bench. "Get up there."

Kiera did as she was told. It put her more leveled with him. It put her ample breasts closer. Eli let his hands roam up her body as he moved closer to her. He took in his mouth one of her chocolate nipples and sucked on it. Kiera moaned as she rubbed his curly hair. She watched him go from the one breast to the other one. He kissed down her torso to where the junction in between her legs began. He ordered her to turn around and bend over. She did anticipating the feel of all that dick he had.

She could feel him rubbing the thick head of his dick against her clit and teasing her opening. *Put it in*, she thought. *Please put it in*. When he did, it was the best feeling. She caught her breath and held it upon his entrance. When he slid outward, Kiera released the breath. "Oh, my...God!"

Kiera's moans could be heard above the forceful sounds of the shower. She had never had dick that felt this damn good. If Eli was like his brother Abe, Kiera could understand why Lovely pranced around so happy all of the time. Eli was rough and aggressive. He fucked her hard and good where she was feeling all of him in her stomach.

Kiera let out a long wail as her pussy walls contracted tightly around Eli convulsively trying to force him out. Kiera's body thrust uncontrollably. Eli released inside of Kiera immediately regretting his actions. "Fuck!"

A satisfied grin spread across Kiera's face. She eased up off his dick and slowly turned toward him. She could tell he was scolding himself internally. "What's wrong Eli?"

"Get out," Eli said without a hint of emotion.

Kiera frowned. "What?"

"You interrupting my goddamn shower. Getcho ass out!" he said.

"You're confusing, you know that?" Kiera said. Her feelings were a bit bruised.

"Yeah, well people in hell want ice water."

"What?" Kiera asked as she burst into laughter.

Eli started laughing too.

"Your ass is retarded." She stared up at him wishing he was hers. He looked back down at her. Kiera could sense there was something different in the way he looked at her. Perhaps he wanted her more than he was willing to admit to. "Why are you looking at me like that?"

Eli replied, "Cause I'm wondering why your monkey ass is still in the shower with me."

Chapter Nine

This was Abe's first time experiencing fatherhood with a brand-new baby. AJ was a very calm quiet baby. Maybe because there was someone always in his face and would pick him up before he cried. He was spoiled. Abe didn't mind. But he wished AJ was on the same schedule as he was. Other than that Abe was enjoying being a father for the first time.

"Here, let me take baby," Lulu offered reaching for AJ. Abe was drifting away to a much-needed state of sleep. He said, "I got it, Lulu."

"No, you don't. I take baby, you sleep," Lulu said pulling the baby from Abe's grasp.

Lovely walked into the family room carrying an empty bottle. "Abe, is AJ sleep yet?"

Lulu chuckled, "AJ put Abe sleep."

"I'm awake," Abe said getting up taking the bottle. "I got that. Go sit down."

"Abe, I can move around," Lovely said watching his frame move away from her.

"Sit down," Abe ordered playfully over his shoulder. He went in the kitchen. Grace was at the breakfast bar stuffing her face with a big bowl of cereal and watching the built-in television on the wall. Abe sometimes wondered about that girl. She was growing like a weed, tall and lanky. She was very athletic. Grace was way mature for her twelve years, and she had the most eccentric personality.

Grace looked up from feeding her face and gave Abe a head nod. "What's up home slice?"

"I can't call it," Abe replied.

"Well check it. I'm 'bout to book it out of here but what's the skinny on that phone?"

"Let me get back at you on that."

"I can dig it," Grace said. She hopped down off her stool. "I'll catch you on the flip side young blood."

Abe laughed while shaking his head. Grace was such a character. She had also watched too many movies from the 70's with Aunt Livy.

Lulu passed by carrying AJ. Abe said, "Here let me take him."

Lulu held AJ away and said, "I have him. You go sit over there with Lovely. Enjoy minute of rest."

"Yes ma'am," Abe chuckled. Thank God for Lulu and Aunt Livy being in the same house. He loved his son, but he didn't know what he would do if they didn't have so much help. A different person had AJ at any given moment that it was a wonder he knew who his true parents were.

Abe sat down beside Lovely who was stretched out on the sofa. She looked tired and disheveled. Her hair had grown to her shoulders but was pulled back in a slovenly gathered ponytail, and her hairline was frizzy. She wore a plain white v-neck t-shirt with a pair of navy gym shorts. She looked so comfortable that Abe decided to lay on her and positioned himself in between her legs. With his head on her chest, he said, "I love you."

"I love you too," she mumbled. She immediately began rubbing his hair. "Abe, are you growing your hair out?"

"I haven't gotten a haircut. I kinda like waking up not worrying about grooming."

Lovely snickered. "So, in other words, you're enjoying being lazy."

"Something like that. But the baby won't let me be too lazy. You know how many diapers I throw out a day?"

Lovely saddened, "But you're going back to work next week."

"It's just part-time. I won't be in the office that much, but I'll work strictly from home if you need me to."

"No baby. I know you miss the office. Four weeks was way more than expected. I appreciate you for it too. You're a wonderful husband and baby daddy."

"Y'all are so freakin corny!" Grace said as she passed through the den.

"Mind your business girl," Abe returned. He smiled inwardly. He said to Lovely, "I gotta admit I love my life. I have a beautiful wife, pretty daughter, a wonderful baby boy. What more could I ask for?"

Lovely smiled, "And don't forget about your new endeavors once the acquisition of the construction company is complete with the BevyCo Corporation."

"You know I feel better with that decision as each day goes by," Abe said. After the merger, Luciano wanted to take the construction business international just as he had done with the resorts and casinos. He also wanted to expand on the realty division of Abe's company.

Lovely said, "And now we can focus on our projects."

"Which is what I've always wanted to concentrate on. Besides going into philanthropy full time will allow me more time to spend with you, AJ, and Grace. Of course, I'll do contract work for BevyCo, but my presence will not be needed as much."

"I know," Lovely said excitedly. "It's going to be so fun working alongside you almost every day." Abe and Lovely both made the decision to go into philanthropy and developing more resources and organizations for low-income families and troubled inner-city kids.

"It's funny how a year ago I wouldn't have thought about being where I am now," Abe said with thought.

"Yeah. You've become a father to two kids in not even a year's time," Lovely chuckled. Abe didn't even bother with adopting Grace. Since she had no father listed on her birth certificate, he and Lovely decided it was easiest if they had her certificate amended to put his name on the certificate as Grace's father. Her name was changed too. She was now Grace Masters.

A year before he had been longing for such a life and agonizing over his past hurts. Since moving forward with Lovely, he have not had a moment that he regretted doing so. He was looking forward to the laid-back life.

There was a knock on the French Doors leading out to the private terrace. Abe went to answer the door.

It was Eric. He began talking right away. "Look dude. My boy just called me from Boston. He said that nigga Lo in some shit. Said that nigga done fucked over some Italians and they want they shit. The word is he done promised these mothafuckas he'd have their money in a few weeks. He just needed to make some moves back in Tennessee."

Abe's eyes quickly went to Lovely on the sofa. Eric lowered his voice and said, "My bad."

Abe led Eric towards the great room. Once they were alone, Abe asked, "He's coming back here?"

"My boy said he been in Tennessee. He go back and forward. They said that mothafucka been talking alotta shit. Said his boys back in Tennessee got his back."

Abe sighed in frustration. "Who the fuck that nigga talking about? Us?"

Eric chuckled, "I guess so."

"I ain't getting between him and the Italians. That's his shit. That nigga need to stay where the fuck he's at."

"You still ain't talk to Lovely?"

"Nah, I don't want to."

"I'll keep a lookout for his ass. He might call me before he call you." Changing to a lighter subject Eric asked, "How's Lovely and that baby?"

"They good. Kam ain't pregnant yet?" Abe asked playfully.

"She bet not be...I'll be kicking her pregnant ass out the house," Eric retorted.

Eric had returned and been serious about living just as clean a lifestyle as Abe. The new location for his luxury car dealership was in the making. And now he and Abe were in the end stages of their urban nightclub, Southern Wild.

This situation with Lorenzo was messing with Abe though. Lorenzo was a troublemaker and a hot head. He was one of those people that hadn't grown up and didn't want to live a normal life. He still ran in the streets wreaking havoc. That was Abe's concern. He didn't want Lorenzo seeing Lovely and getting any ideas. Abe would hate to have to bring out his alter ego Fyah, but he would if it was necessary.

Abe approached Lovely on the sofa. "Lovely?"

"Yes?" she said softly.

"I'll be back okay. I promise I won't be long, but I gotta take care of something."

"You're fine. Just make sure you come home to us," she said.

He leaned down and kissed her softly on the lips. "I love you, lady."

"I love you too, guy."

Lovely sometimes wondered about Abe and his different personalities. Was he aware of how he transitioned from one to another? He didn't use the word nigga habitually but when he held conversations with street guys he did. And who was he talking about anyway?

Abe left with Eric. He had to see what the word on the street was.

———

Lovely was bothered which was unusual. Lovely always tried to maintain her composure and mask her troubles. She would smile through the storm when inside she was actually sad. Seldom did she want to impose her worries onto anyone else.

Lately, Lovely had been feeling the need to unearth her desire to bring to justice those that took her sight, violated her, and killed her parents. A long time ago when it happened, she banished the idea of pursuing her assailants for fear of them coming after her. Now, however, she felt safer than she had ever felt having someone like Abe in her life.

"What's wrong with you?" Robin asked as she plopped down on the sofa beside her.

"Nothing," Lovely mumbled. She continued to look towards the television. She started to feel vulnerable and in need of her husband's attention. Lovely grabbed her cell phone from the coffee table. She spoke into her Bluetooth device, "Call Abe."

Abe answered eagerly, "Lovely?"

Lovely got up and began to walk toward her great room. "Hey. What are you doing?"

"Nothing. Sitting here with my brothers and Eric. What's up?"

"You're not with your girlfriend, are you?"

"Girlfriend? What I look like having a girlfriend and your ass?"

"You would be worn out," Lovely snickered. "So how long will you be there?"

"You need me home baby?" he teased. "I can come home."

"I'm horny."

"Oh, you don't have to worry about that. I got you. How many rounds you wanna go?"

Lovely laughed. "You're crazy. Just make sure you don't get caught up doing something and lose track of time."

"Even if I did get home late I know how to wake you up."

"Oh yeah? And how is that?"

"You know you love it; being woke up with all this dick girl."

"All of what dick? Boy bye!"

Abe chuckled. "I'll be home in about an hour. Okay?"

"That's fine." Lovely heard the doorbell rang. "Hold on. Someone is at the door."

"Let Lulu answer it."

"I am," Lovely said.

"Where's my daughter and son?"

"Down in your man cave with Aunt Livy."

"What? Aunt Livy is downstairs? That's a first. You know this is crazy. My brother wants me to leave but I coulda sworn this was still my house."

"Eli ain't being like that is he?" Lovely said. Her ears tuned into the female voice floating in from the foyer.

"He's being mean to me."

Robin walked into the great room from the foyer. "Lovely, Ms. Sarah is here."

Lovely looked in their direction and could make out the figure of a slender built lady behind Robin. Lovely said to Abe, "Hey let me call you back. Your mother is here."

"My what? What she doing there?"

"I don't know. I'll call you back," Lovely said ending the call. She stood to greet Sarah with a hug. "Sarah, to what do I owe the pleasure?"

"I was hoping to catch Abe here. I needed to speak to him about something."

"I was just on the phone with him cause he's not here," Lovely said. "He's actually at Eli's right now."

"I will go there after I leave here. So how have you been?"

"I've been good. How about you?"

"I'm doing well," she answered.

"Have a seat. Can Lulu get you anything?"

"Oh no. I'm fine," Sarah said sitting in the chair. She looked around taking in the eloquence of the home. "I still can't get over how Abe did this house."

"He's good. Did you know he was talented like that as a kid?" Lovely asked. This question wasn't genuine. Lovely wanted to see how Sarah answered it. Lovely was aware of the abuse Abe underwent as a child from both Sarah and his stepfather Esau.

"I knew he was smart, so becoming an architect was not surprising. What was surprising was him obtaining a doctorate's. I didn't know he was that serious. I'm amazed he doesn't use his title more often though."

"Well you know Abe isn't very formal. That street mentality still dwells in him. He's very lackadaisical in his demeanor. I think that's one of the reasons I love him so much."

"You two are really in love huh?" Sarah chuckled.

Lovely smiled. "We are. As a person, I like him and adore him. He's very amiable in his own right. I would be fine with just being his friend. But as my man, I love the hell out of him."

"I getcha," Sarah smiled back.

Lovely asked, "So will you be making amends with Abe soon? You know he would love it. And it would make his whole year. Having you in his life would mean so much to him, you know that don't you?"

Sarah nodded. "Yeah. I know. That's what I want to do tonight. So, with that being said, I need to get to Eli's house. But before I do that let me go see my grandson. He's the first grandbaby."

Lovely led Sarah downstairs where Sarah spent about ten minutes adoring her grandson.

Lovely grinned excitedly. "Oh, I'm so excited about you and Abe." Lovely walked Sarah to the front door. Robin who was standing back in the kitchen's butler's pantry followed behind Lovely. Sarah said goodbye and left. As she was driving down to the iron gate, a black Charger with dark tints entered when the gate opened.

"Are you expecting company?" Robin asked.

"Nope. I wasn't even expecting Sarah," Lovely said.

"It's a black Charger," Robin said standing by the door eyeing the car as it pulled up along the front of the house. She felt as if she had seen that car before.

Lovely gave it some thought. "I don't know who that could be."

The passenger door opened and out stepped a nice-looking guy dressed in all white. He had a nice curly afro. He grinned at Robin. "Ay, Abe in there?"

"No. Who are you?" Robin asked. There was something oddly familiar about him. Robin couldn't put her finger on it though.

"Lorenzo. I'm his cousin. That was my aunt that just left wasn't it? She didn't even know it was me," he laughed. He asked, "You ain't Lovely, are you?"

"No," Robin said. "She's in here though. You wanna speak to her?"

Lorenzo said something to the people in the car before he ascended the steps to the house. "What's up? What's your name ma?"

Robin side-eyed him, "I'm Robin." She stepped aside to let Lorenzo inside.

Like everyone else, Lorenzo took a moment to take in the majestic interior of the house. He said, "This a bad mothafucka. Abe living like this now?"

"How can I help you?" Lovely asked standing in the entryway to the hallways separating the dining room from the foyer.

Lorenzo's eyes fell on Lovely, and he immediately recognized her. His dick grew hard as he remembered thirteen years ago how she fought under his hold as he took her young virginal innocence. "Are you Lovely?"

"Yes, I am. You said you're Abe's cousin?"

"Yeah Lorenzo. I came by to speak to Abe. Rosalyn said he ain't here, but I wanted—"

"Robin," Lovely corrected.

"Yeah, Robin said he ain't here," Lorenzo said looking Lovely up and down. The navy gym shorts she was wearing fit snug to her body. They did nothing to obscure the curviness of her build. He said, "Abe know he can get ahold of some fine ass women."

Lovely wasn't flattered. She said, "Abe isn't here, but I can give you his number if you don't have it."

"I got it. I thought I'd just stop by since we fam'ly and all." Lorenzo shot Robin a look and gave her a quick wink.

"Yeah," Lovely said. "Well give him a call, and I'm sure he'll meet you. Lorenzo, it was nice to meet you. Robin, will you lock up after he leaves?"

Lovely headed to her master suite. She shut the door and locked it behind her. Something about him didn't sit right with her. His voice eerily reminded her of the night of the home invasion. It was rough and raspy just like one of her assailants. She called Abe again.

Abe whispered, "Hey baby. Guess who just came here?"

"Your mama?"

"Yep. She said she talked with you for a little bit."

Lovely was thrilled that Abe was in the presence of his mother, but she wasn't trying to discuss that at the moment. "Uhm...your cousin is here looking for you."

"What cousin?"

"Lorenzo."

Abe's whole tone changed. "Lovely, don't let him in the house. I'm on my way right now. I mean it. Don't let that mothafucka in the house."

"He's already in here. Robin is seeing him out."

"Shit—where are you, the baby and Grace?"

"I'm in the bedroom. They're still downstairs with Aunt Livy."

"Go down there and take them upstairs to Livy's apartment. I'm on my way."

He hung up. This alarmed Lovely. She grew nervous and wasn't sure if she should even step out of the room, but the elevator was just right around the corner. Doing as Abe ordered, Lovely eased out into the hallway. She could hear Lorenzo was still talking to Robin. Lovely got on the elevator and went down to the lower floor and did as Abe told her.

———

Robin's ill feelings towards Lovely had deepened. Why couldn't she have the life Lovely had? It was fine being the assistant, but lately Lovely didn't even call on Robin to do anything for her. She called on Aunt Livy, Lulu, Jackie when she was in town, and even Kiera. Why was Kiera trying to get in good with Lovely and Abe now?

Grant it, Grace and the twins hung out together, and Kiera had business with Abe now, but from what Robin remembered Lovely wasn't too fond of Kiera. When did that change? She liked the bitch now because she was doing her hair? What was it?

Then there was Eli's attitude. Why couldn't he act right and be like his brother? His elusiveness drove Robin further

139

into her lover's arms. If Robin didn't know better, she would think Eli and Kiera had something going on. She wasn't sure, so she didn't point any fingers just yet.

"You're bothered."

Snapping out of her thoughts Robin turned to her lover. "I was just lost in my thoughts."

"Do you care to share?"

"Not really."

He sighed and stared up at the ceiling and fell into his own deep thoughts.

"Now you're bothered. What is it, baby?"

"Money."

Robin turned her head away from him, so he wouldn't see her rolling her eyes. Money was always an issue with him. Robin thought of how fat her bank account had gotten over the past seven months only for him to deplete it all in need of favors. When Robin first started helping herself to Lovely's funds, her goal was to have enough money so that she could live as fabulous as the celebrities on television. Letting him know what she was doing had been a mistake.

Robin asked, "What is it now?"

"I have debts, Robin."

"Okay. I'm moving money. The account should be back up in a couple of months."

"It's not fast enough. Besides you're only able to do it in little amounts."

"If I do bigger amounts it will raise a red flag," Robin said.

He remained quiet as his mind began working overtime.

140

"What are you thinking baby?" Robin asked.

He turned toward her and wrapped his arm around her. "Are you ready to be rich? You can stop stealing from Lovely."

"Of course."

"Well, I have an idea. I just gotta go over some specifics with my partner."

Robin nodded. "Okay. What do you have in mind?"

"I'll fill you in on it later. Just know that you will have a big part in it."

———

Melissa was definitely a confused woman. She laid lazily in bed as her husband massaged her feet. Reggie hadn't pampered her in years. He was really trying this time. Melissa moaned, "Ah! This feels like heaven."

"You deserve it."

Melissa smiled. She asked, "Do you want me to do you next?"

"No. You just lay here and relax. There's something I wanna talk to you about though."

"What?" Melissa asked feeling alarmed.

"Now before I start speaking I want you to have an open mind to what I'm about to say," Reggie said still rubbing her feet.

"What is it?"

"I was thinking we should move to Knoxville."

Melissa's mouth hung open. She was flabbergasted. "What?"

"Let's move to Knoxville baby," he repeated.

"How long have you been thinking about this?" Melissa asked.

"For a while now," he said.

"I don't know."

"I said have an open mind. We already have a place to live. Even you said my mama's basement apartment was nice."

"Wait. You wanna live with your mama?" Melissa said. She pulled her feet away from his grip.

"Technically it's not living with her."

"It's her house," Melissa argued.

"But it's separate Melissa. It even has its own electric meter."

"But we have this house, Reggie. What do you suppose we do with this house?"

"Sell it."

"What about income? Where will I be able to find a job that will pay me as good as Abe does?"

"You'll find a job. Besides living with Mama will cut down on our monthly expenses."

"I can't leave Abe like that."

Reggie shook his head. He grew agitated quickly. "There you go with that Abe shit. He'll find someone to replace you. Hell, he'll do it and won't think two shits about you."

Melissa gave it some thought. "Let me think over it some more baby."

"Don't take too long thinking."

"I won't," she said. Maybe a change of scenery could be what their marriage needed to get it back on the right track. Melissa would definitely give it more thought.

Reggie went back into loving mode. He grabbed Melissa's foot and kissed it. "There's one more thing."

"What is it?"

"I need to help my sister out back home. She going through a hard time. I was wondering if I could take six thousand out of the account to help her out."

"Six thousand?" she asked in disbelief.

"Yeah. Well, I was gonna help my mama out too." He kissed her feet again.

How much helping did they need? Six thousand? Melissa didn't want to voice her reluctance to help. He would accuse her of being a "selfish fat bitch" as he always did. She wanted to show him she was willing to give him her all if he was willing to change. She said, "Sure."

Chapter Ten

A few days later after Abe returned from his paternity break, he found himself working diligently on a 3-D model for Luciano's proposed mountain resort. Abe got a knock on his office suite door. "Yes?"

Felicia, the receptionist, stepped in. "Abe, you have a visitor. Said he really needs to see you."

"Who?" Abe asked.

Before Felicia could tell him, Lorenzo eased by her. "'Scuse me, Miss Lady. Abe! What up nigga?"

Abe tried to keep his composure, but it was hard. Abe gestured toward one of the chairs on the other side of his desk. "Have a seat."

Felicia gave Abe a questioning look to see what he wanted to do. Abe gave her a subtle nod to let her know he was okay. Felicia left shutting the door behind her.

Abe asked, "So what can I do for you?"

Lorenzo looked at the model Abe had been working on. "So, this the shit you do all day? Arts and crafts nigga?"

"I'm putting together a scaled 3-D model of what we'll be working on by later this year. I don't do the arts and crafts part of this business all day. I do have a construction crew, and I do have property to oversee. Are you interested in this line of business?" Abe asked keeping his attitude professional. "I could always use the extra help."

"Maybe," Lorenzo said looking around Abe's upscale and contemporarily designed office. "You doing the thing though. First your house and your office. This whole office building bad."

"Yeah, speaking of my house. You do know not to ever take your ass there again, right?" Abe asked starting to unravel.

"I figured you might say that. So, let's just say I'll respect that."

"What do you want?" Abe asked losing his patience.

"I need some money. You know get up on my feet and live like you living my nigga."

"Ant ain't helping you out in that department?"

"Fuck Antino. I'm asking you, cousin."

"What are you talking about exactly?"

"I don't know...maybe two-fifty."

"Hundred?"

"Nah nigga. Thousand."

"You want me to hand you two hundred fifty thousand dollars just like that?"

Lorenzo shrugged casually. "Why not?"

"Why not?" Abe asked with disbelief.

"Yeah. We fam'ly. You know I ain't got much of shit. I just wanna come up like you and how we used to do in the day."

"Yeah, I remember that," Abe mumbled.

"Give me about a week and let me hit you back up about working for you too."

The door opened and in walked Eli and Ike. They were already on alert. Ike looked at Lorenzo and said, "Hey Lo."

"What's up cuz," Lorenzo mumbled. He looked back at Abe. "You gon' help me out?"

Abe said, "What if I can't?"

Lorenzo gave him a doubtful look. "Are you serious? You got money coming outcho ass nigga."

"Well, what if I say I don't want to?"

"Why wouldn't you want to help me out? We used to be partners in crime."

"That was yesterday. This is a new day Lorenzo," Abe said. "A lot of shit I done then I don't do anymore."

Lorenzo sat back in his chair and looked long at Abe. A wicked smile began to spread across Lorenzo's face. "I know something about you."

Abe grimaced with a slight shrug, "I don't give a damn about whatchu know."

Lorenzo chuckled, "Why you so uptight Abe."

"I know you, Lo," Abe said. He shook his head. "You be on that bullshit."

"Maybe I do. But you on that bullshit for what you're doing."

"And what is that?"

"So, your new lady is Mano's niece. Interesting," Lorenzo said with a smirk.

Abe's brow furrowed. Ike and Eli could see Abe tense up as his jaws clenched. Ike inched closer to the desk just in case it didn't provide enough of a barrier between Abe and Lorenzo.

Abe stared coldly at Lorenzo. "Why does that even concern you?"

"You the one that should be concern. I mean, don't you think it's kinda fucked up?"

Eli could see that Abe was seconds away from beating Lorenzo's ass. He said, "Lo, I think you really need to just get on up outta here."

Lorenzo stared at Abe as he said, "Not until Abe understands our agreement."

"What agreement?" Abe asked.

"My money," Lorenzo said with a vindictive grin. He went on to say, "You and I both know that you're gonna give me that money. After all what price can you put on that beautiful thang Lovely?"

Abe shot up from his seat and hovered over his desk, "Don't speak Lovely's name from your mouth!"

Lorenzo laughed. "You know I still remember how tight her pussy was when I was tearing that—"

As Eli feared, Abe leaped over that desk in one quick movement and was on Lorenzo. It amazed Eli that Abe could move so quick for his large frame. And Eli wasn't going to intervene. Abe needed to beat Lorenzo's ass for what he was saying.

The noise alerted the others in the building. Fortunately, Abe's uncles were in the building and ran into the room to help Ike separate the two men.

Felicia was at the door. "Do we need to call the police?"

Lorenzo tore away from Uncle Larry. He had a busted lip and under his left eye had begun to swell already. "Let me the fuck go! I'll leave but remember mu'fucka who you fucking wit!"

"No, I think you done forgot who the fuck you just fucked with," Abe returned. "Get the fuck out my office! Don't bring your stupid ass back around here or my house again!"

Lorenzo pushed passed everyone angrily as he made his way out of Abe's office. Uncle Larry followed to make sure he left.

"What in the world?" Uncle Paul asked in shock.

"Nothing Unc," Eli said shaking his head. He looked over at the model Abe had been working on. It was upside down on the floor. *What a shame*, Eli thought. Now Abe would have to salvage what he could and basically start all over.

––––––––

Lorenzo's visit had Abe peeved. It sent him right back to where he was after Eric came to visit seven months ago; anxious and terrified that Lovely would learn the truth. He couldn't let it happen. He even had urges to do things that Fyah would have done just to make sure Lovely didn't learn the truth. Abe felt himself suppressing those feelings as if he was Bruce Banner trying to prevent the onset of The Hulk.

He couldn't wait to be home. Being around all of the ladies and his little man provided him a comfort that seemed to always put him at ease.

Grace, Lulu and Aunt Livy were in the kitchen when Abe made his way inside the house. Grace grinned announcing, "And the king is here!"

Abe smiled. "So that makes you the princess huh?"

"Naw, I'm the jester. It suits me better," Grace giggled.

"Oh, be quiet with your silly butt," Aunt Livy said swatting at Grace.

Grace ducked and went up to Abe. "Hey, you convince Mama that I need my own phone yet?"

"I don't think she's going for it," Abe said. He looked down at Grace and admired how pretty she was. Her long jet-black hair flowed down her back in deep waves. She was tall with a slim build. She had the same heart-shaped face as Lovely. Her lips were even the same shape as Lovely's. It was a good thing Grace looked so much like Lovely rather than Lorenzo, but the resemblance was still there.

"Man, I really need a phone," Grace whined. "An iPhone to be exact."

"I'll see if I can talk to her some more," Abe said. That was one of the things Abe appreciated about Lovely. She didn't feel a need to be frivolous with her money and do things just because she could. Lovely could afford to buy a million iPhones for Grace, but that didn't supersede her parenting and the lesson she was teaching her daughter. She was very modest with her lifestyle. The only thing Abe saw Lovely invest so much in was her house. Her nine-bedroom mansion was grand and well-designed. No expense was spared in making it the spectacular home that it was. Abe loved it, especially his lower level man cave.

Lulu didn't appreciate Abe's unsolicited taste testing of her chicken and rice dish. She slapped his hand when he went for a second bite. "No double dip!"

Grace laughed. "She popped you!"

"Shut up," Abe said playfully. He asked, "Where's your mama?"

"She's laying down while AJ is sleeping," Grace said.

"Let me go check on my babies," he said. He went into the bedroom he shared with Lovely. The television was on, but Lovely was buried under the covers. Abe sat down on the edge of the bed where Lovely was.

Lovely mumbled, "Get outta here Grace."

"It's not Grace," Abe chuckled.

Lovely folded the covers back from her face. She was wearing a joyful smile. "You're home!"

Mocking her excitement, he said, "I'm home!"

Lovely sat up and opened her arms up to him. Abe wrapped his arms around her holding her tight. He kissed her softly on the lips.

Lovely returned his kiss. "Abe," she spoke softly.

"Yes, baby."

"Would you ever hurt me on purpose?"

"Of course not."

"I wouldn't hurt you on purpose either. But what if there were things about me that you didn't know and once you found out it would make you feel different about me?"

"Like what Lovely?" That question cause Abe's heart to thump wildly in his chest. What a coincidence for her to ask a question like that not realizing Abe was going through that very thing.

"I don't know. Like what if you found out I slept with Eli?"

Abe laughed. "Really?"

"Why is that funny?"

"That was the worst example you could have used. My brother knows better than to cross me like that."

Lovely snickered. "Okay. What if I stole all of your money?"

Abe was thankful that Lovely couldn't see the sudden change of his expression. Why was she bringing this up? Where was she going with this? It made him uncomfortable. Remaining at ease, he cautiously answered, "You can have all of my money. I wouldn't even care."

Lovely hit him playfully. "Give me a realistic answer."

"That is. Lovely, I don't care about nothing else as long as I'm with you, AJ and Grace."

"Well, what could you possibly found out about me that would be a no go?"

Remembering how angry Lorenzo's visit made him, Abe said, "Joining forces with my enemies I guess. That would hurt more than anything. I would look at you differently. That would tell me that your love for me was never genuine."

"Just so you know Abe, my love is genuine. I wouldn't want you to think anything different."

"Baby, I know. You don't have to tell me. I feel it. I feel it when we make love and how you greet me every evening when I come home. I feel it in the way you touch me and how you kiss me. I feel it when you cry when you cum. I love that shit...I love you." He kissed her tenderly on the lips. He said, "I love that you had my child. You gave me a son."

"So, you love that I'm your baby mama?" she asked playfully.

Abe replied, "You are not a baby mama. You're my wife and the mother of my child."

Lovely joked, "Well you just my baby daddy!"

Chapter Eleven

R obin was on her way to Lovely's when she suddenly felt an urge to go visit Eli since his house was the fourth street before Lovely's. Pulling up to the gate Robin entered the code into the keypad and the gates opened for her. She rode up the winding driveway. She parked under the portico.

She got out and started ringing the doorbell and knocked. Within minutes Eli was opening the door. When he saw her, his expression became blank. "Come in," he said stepping aside for Robin.

She stepped into his foyer. He gestured for her to go first up the winding staircase to the main floor. Once they got to the landing, Eli asked, "What are you doing here so early?"

"I was on my way back to Lovely's, and I thought I would stop by," she said.

"Well, come on to the den," he said.

Robin took a seat on the sofa in the den. Eli sat down next to her. "So, what exactly brings you here?"

"I wanted to see you," Robin said.

"Well I feel so honored," he said a bit amused.

Robin eyed Eli up and down, "So what's up?"

"You tell me."

"Why did it seem like things between us went downhill after we slept with each other?"

Eli's immediate response was to shrug his shoulders. Then he thought about it. He said, "Maybe because you were pushing for something I wasn't ready for."

"Don't try to put this on me," Robin said in defense mode.

"I'm not putting it all on you. But I did express to you that I wanted to take things slow Robin."

"How slow did it have to be?"

"Just until I knew I wanted to commit to a monogamous relationship," Eli explained genuinely.

"So, the whole time we've been doing...whatever this is, you've been seeing other people?"

There was no sense in lying about it. Eli nodded his head.

Robin shook her head with disgust. "Who?"

"Do it really matter who?"

"A man? Just tell me if it was with a man," Robin asked desperately. "Are you really bisexual?"

Eli stared at Robin blankly. Why was his sexuality in question? Eli used to find it amusing but lately it was annoying the fuck out of him. Shit, he and Robin had been fucking for the past seven months off and on, and she still hadn't figured it out.

Eli shook his head with disbelief. "Look, I'm about to head over to Abe's."

"So, you don't wanna finish this talk?" Robin asked.

"No, I really don't," he said with irritation as he got up.

"Just like that?"

"Yep. Are you coming with me? Weren't you on your way home anyway?"

Robin blew air in aggravation. Frustrated, she abruptly got up and headed toward the staircase.

Eli didn't care about her feelings right about now. He was tired of talking about the same damn thing. He told her over and over he wasn't ready for anything exclusive. He didn't like the idea of constantly lying. He definitely didn't like the idea of answering to anybody. Robin had become aggressive and demanding. Eli wasn't with that. She wasn't running anything.

They drove in their separate cars to Abe and Lovely's house. When they got their Eli noticed Kiera's car parked in the front courtyard. Eli was not expecting to see Kiera there. It threw Eli completely off. Kiera was becoming increasingly attractive to Eli. He found himself wanting to reenact the lovemaking scene they had a couple of weeks ago. He couldn't take his mind off of it. Even being with Robin didn't erase thoughts of Kiera. However, Eli knew he couldn't go down that road again with Kiera. She was poisonous. He couldn't get caught up in her games.

"Hey Eli," Kiera smiled.

"Hey," he said quietly.

Confused by her presence Eli asked, "Why are you here?"

Kiera grinned, "Bria and Bryce wanted to come over and see Grace and AJ."

Eli wasn't sure what that grin was for, but he could tell Kiera was being conniving.

Abe added, "And she's here so she and I can discuss business."

"What kind of business?" Robin asked eyeing Kiera keenly.

Kiera cut her eyes. "Is it really your business?"

Robin said, "I guess not."

Just realizing Abe was present Eli asked, "Where's Lovely?"

"She's asleep," Abe said. "The baby is wearing her out."

"Is she worn out from AJ or have you put another one in the oven already?" Kiera teased.

Abe laughed a little. "I hope she would tell me if that was the case."

"You never know with Lovely. She'll sprang the news on you when you least expect it, Abe," Eli said.

Robin watched Eli interact especially with Kiera. What Robin didn't like was Eli's total disregard for her presence.

When Robin had joined Aunt Livy and Lulu in the kitchen, Kiera took the opportunity to say in a low whisper to Eli, "Get rid of her and let me come to your house tonight."

"Hell naw!"

"Please?" Kiera pleaded.

Eli shook his head emphatically. "I can't go there with you again."

"Why not? Didn't you enjoy it?"

"I did but...," his voice trailed as his eyes landed on Robin. Eli wasn't sure if Robin was trying to come back to his house or not. The way he was feeling she could take her ass somewhere else.

"You really like that bitch huh?" Kiera asked. Kiera wished she could tell Eli the truth about the company he was keeping.

Eli sarcastically said, "Yeah, just about as much as I like your bitch ass."

"Why you so mean to me, Eli?"

Eli side eyed her. "Cause you can't be trusted."

"Me? Why you think I'm some bad ass person?"

Eli said, "You are. Why you don't wanna get no DNA test?"

"So that's what this is about? How many times do I gotta tell you?"

"I need to see it on paper."

Kiera looked up and saw Robin shooting daggers Kiera's way as she walked back over to Eli. Kiera looked at Eli, "Well we'll discuss that some other time."

Eli's eyes went to Kiera's ass as she walked away. He knew he wouldn't mind getting into that ass that night. So, at the last minute, he said, "Kiera...I'll text you."

Kiera looked back and grinned sneakily. She ignored Robin's stare. "Alright."

Robin looked at Eli, "Text her what?"

"There you go," Eli said in aggravation. "It doesn't concern you."

Robin left it alone. It wasn't really Eli she was concerned about. It was making sure Kiera stayed in line.

———

Lovely couldn't sleep. Lovely had dreamt about the night of the invasion thirteen years ago. She was being raped and crying. She wanted her father to save her, but he was unable to. In her dream, her father was already dead hanging from the ceiling beside her mother hanging from the ceiling. They both dangled in the air with big holes in their foreheads. In her dream, Lovely was not blindfolded. She could see her parents. She could see the invaders. Two of them had blank faces, but the one face was clear. He had a tatted arm of demonic creatures all up and down from his wrist to his shoulder.

"Why this bitch's blindfold off?" And in a split second, he hit her. "Don't fucking look at me!"

In the dream, Lovely's eyes were slit open after she got a good look at one of her assailants. She screamed over and over. He said, "Kill that bitch!" The gun went off.

Lovely sat up in bed lightly perspiring. She looked around the room and could see that it was dark. How long had she slept? She didn't intend to sleep so long but lately, she had been exhausted.

She felt around for her phone until she found it under her pillow. She spoke into it. "Call Mano."

Seconds later a South Indian accented voice answered, "Lovely?"

"Yeah, it's me," she said sounding disheartened.

"What is wrong?"

"I think I need to know now," Lovely said. She sighed, "I've been thinking...I think I'm ready to move forward."

Mano chuckled, "Are you sure? I want to know who was responsible for my brother's death also, but it's been many years."

"Well didn't you say you had connections in that department?" Lovely asked.

"I know people, yes."

"And you said if I wanted to, you could find out who did this to me and who killed my parents. Right?"

"Yes," Mano said.

"And you said you had people that could handle them."

"Yes, but what do you plan to do with this information Lovely?"

"I don't know. What I said I'd always do. Make them pay. But I'm sure they're probably somewhere in a prison doing time for other crimes they've committed."

"Are you sure this is what you want?"

"Mano, you know people that could take care of them, right?"

"Yeah but Lovely..."

"No buts. I've put this off long enough."

"Why now?"

"I'm having the dreams again," she said softly, almost ashamed to admit.

"Oh, I see."

"I think I need closure. I never got that. None of them have been brought to justice for what they done to me."

"I understand."

"Hopefully they're dead," she said without remorse.

"Maybe they are. But if they're not and find out, you're alive and you know who they are they'll come after you first. That's why I said it was dangerous for you to go back there in the first place."

"Well, it's too late to turn back now. I wanna move forward."

"I want you to be careful about all of this. Don't approach nobody without my men or me with you."

"I understand. Abe will kill me if he knew what I was up to."

"Don't tell him yet," Mano said. "He'll be doing what any husband would do. He would just want to protect you."

"I know. And Mano, do not tell Cesar or Luciano what I'm doing," Lovely said.

He was hesitant in his answer.

"Mano!"

"Alright, alright," he finally said. "I won't tell."

"You promise?"

"Lovely, shouldn't they know? I mean Lu lives there now and who better to look after you than him?"

"But Lu overreacts," Lovely said. She sighed. "Okay, don't let them know yet."

"Okay."

"Good. Give Raja and those grandbabies of yours my love."

"I will. Oh. I will be in the states there to meet with Lu on business. I will come to visit you and your family."

"That sounds great. I look forward to it."

After the call ended Lovely laid back and stared out into nothingness. The room was dark and cool. The sounds of the ceiling fans whirring above were soothing. Lovely laid on her back in the oversized custom-made bed she shared with Abe. Her eyes were closed. Even when she heard the door opening she didn't bother to open her eyes. She felt him crawl into bed with her. She moaned in pure bliss as Abe's hands rubbed and massaged every part of her body.

He whispered, "How does that feel?"

"It feels wonderful," Lovely said with a smile.

Abe admired the curvature of her half-dressed body. She wore only a white cami with her panties. He leaned down and placed soft kisses on her stomach working his way up to her full breasts. Her nipples stood at attention, very hard and rigid. Lovely gasped when he raised her top, and he took the left one in his mouth and began sucking and nibbling. Her hands went to his head and began rubbing his hair.

Abe gave her right breast equal attention before he kissed across her clavicles and to her neck. He asked, "Do you love me?"

Lovely opened her eyes wishing she could see him. "Of course, I do."

"I love you so much," he whispered as he kissed her on the lips.

"I feel you getting sensitive. What's the matter, Abe?"

Abe smiled. "Nothing. I just get this way when I realize how blessed I am to have you."

Lovely smiled back. "I'm blessed to have you. I wouldn't want it any other way."

Abe laid on his side and continued to caress Lovely's body. He reached her pussy easing his hand inside her panties and sticking his finger inside her. Lovely widened her legs like the obedient girl she always was. Abe tickled her clit with the juices from inside her. He felt her love button hardening under his fingers. "This pussy always hot and ready."

"Mmm hmm," Lovely moaned.

"Your ass always wanna fuck."

"Mmm hmm."

"Can I have it?"

"Mmm hmm."

Abe was tickled as he stared at Lovely's face. Her eyes were closed again. She moved her lower half in a circular motion thrusting back onto his fingers. *Hot ass*, he thought. He asked, "Do you want this dick?"

Lovely nodded, "Uh-huh."

Abe placed a kiss on her stomach. He asked, "Can I taste it first?"

"Yes," she moaned as he continued to pump his fingers in and out of her. He stopped long enough to slide her panties off of her. He went back to fingering her. He never stopped as he began swirling his tongue against her hardened clit. Lovely's breathing labored, and she gripped the sheets on either side of her. "Yes! Yes, nigga shit!"

Abe didn't let up with slurping the nectar that flowed from Lovely until she was shaking and calling out to God. He waited until she was done having her sexual seizure before he asked, "How do you want the dick, baby?"

"Just put it in," Lovely moaned.

"Hold them legs up for me," he said quietly. Lovely held her legs high to the ceiling. She needed deep penetration. He wasted no time rubbing his dick head in between the slits of her pussy lips and inside of her. He worked himself inside her with two deep strokes. On the third one, he just let it sit inside her as he enjoyed her muscles tightening around him.

"Baby come on!" Lovely whined. Abe grinned wickedly. He loved teasing her.

Lovely let out an unintelligible sound as she took the length of him. Abe bent her legs back further until her knees were at her shoulders. He kissed her breast and placed kisses on her neck. "You ready?" he asked.

Lovely nodded in anticipation of the torture he was about to put on her. She loved it when he delivered the pain. It felt so damn good. It just didn't feel like good fucking if she didn't let Abe pound it from time to time. It was the most exhilarating feeling, and Lovely loved it.

With every thrust, Lovely hollered and braced herself for the pleasure filled pain that Abe gave to her. When Lovely would push on him, he would pin her arms back by the wrists. He snapped on her, "This is what the fuck you want ain't it?"

"Yes!"

"Then keep them goddamn hands back."

Lovely giggled. She loved this man. No way could she imagine Abe doing any wrong. He was perfect.

About thirty minutes later Abe was spent. He collapsed on top of Lovely. She could feel his skin was moist from perspiration. Their breathing hadn't gotten under control. He laid there on top of her listening to the rapid beats of her heart. Her hand began to rub his head lovingly.

Abe finally moved beside her. He held her close and entwined his legs with hers. He kissed the top of her head and said, "I love your ass so much."

"I love you too baby," Lovely said snuggling his arms closer to her.

Chapter Twelve

A few weeks later Eric was hosting a Labor Day weekend all-white party at Southern Wild. Kiera found herself becoming excited as she got herself dressed for the night. She was looking forward to the night. After all, she was attending as Eli's official date.

Things between her and Eli were gradually turning into a decent relationship. She wasn't his girlfriend of course, but Kiera could see it heading in that direction. Eli wasn't pressuring her anymore about the paternity of the twins, but he would bring it up every now and then, still insisting that he was their father.

Thinking of their father made Kiera apprehensive. He was a mistake she wished she could erase from her life. He was difficult to deal with. The only reason she had anything to do with him was because of money. And he was tight with his money. Sometimes when he didn't want to give up any money, he would deny that he was the twins' father.

Kiera dialed the twins' father. She didn't expect him to answer. He likely would be mad that she was even calling his phone.

"Hello?"

Surprised, Kiera said, "Well this is a surprise. I didn't expect you to actually answer."

"I'll hang up then."

"No! You don't have to."

He sighed with a hint of annoyance. "What do you want Kiera?"

"Why do I call you E? Money! What else?"

"You got money. Your shop doing good business."

"Yeah, but the twins are your kids too."

"Are they?"

Kiera rolled her eyes. "Here you go with this shit. What is it now? You can't say you're broke. I know you got it."

"How you know what the fuck I got?" he asked with an edge.

"Bitch, you got it!" Kiera snapped.

"And this is why I don't like dealing with your belligerent ghetto ass."

There was silence between them. Whenever they spoke, it always turned into a verbal battle. Both would somehow manage to put their pride aside and succumb to a civilized level before the conversation ended.

Kiera turned it down a notch. "So, what's with the attitude?"

"Just got a lot on my mind," he said.

Kiera smirked, "Like what?"

"Just some shit."

Kiera wanted to get in his business. He was always so calm and cool like he had the world under control. He was usually arrogant and getting smart with her. His tone seemed worried. Kiera thought she would toy with him since that's what she was known for doing. "So, how's your love life?"

"Fucked up if you must know. Why do you always wanna know about my love life?"

Kiera chuckled, "Things must not be good with the missus."

"Fuck her," he spat.

"What has she done now?"

"What hasn't she done? I'm sick of dealing with the bitch."

"Then get a divorce. Haven't I been telling you that for years?"

He sighed shaking his head. "It's not that damn simple."

"What? You don't want her walking away with everything?"

"Hell no."

"As much as she has put up with you; she deserves something."

He didn't respond.

Kiera noted the time and realize she was running late for the party. "Well, we need to meet up one day soon. I need my payment."

"You'll get your money," he mumbled with defeat.

"I'll be calling you if I don't hear from you."

"I know you will. Bye Kiera."

Kiera didn't bother with telling him "bye," she simply hung up. She quickly dialed Eli.

He answered, "Yes?"

"Hey!" she said trying to sound cheerful. "What are you doing?"

"I'm getting ready for the party. Am I picking you up?" Eli asked.

"Yeah."

"What's wrong? You sounding kind of funny?"

"Oh, I'm fine. I'll be waiting for you."

Eli said, "Okay, give me thirty minutes."

————

When Kiera and Eli arrived at Southern Wild, the crowd was already lively for its Labor Day party. She saw Lovely and Kam first and latched onto them. She said, "Hey Lovely and Kam!"

"Hey Kiera," Lovely said cheerfully.

Kiera frowned. She asked, "Where's Abe an'nem?"

"Doing some business," she said.

"How he gon leave you here alone? I'ma get him when I see him," Kiera said playfully.

"Please do 'cause I've been here without him long enough," Lovely said.

"I'm missing Eric too," Kam added quietly.

Kiera stared at Eli. Every bit of him was delectable. He had let his facial hair grow in enough for a pencil thin chinstrap beard perfectly lined along with his goatee. He had cut his hair low like Abe's, but instead of it lying flat it swirled with curls and waves. He wasn't wearing the eyebrow piercing or lip piercing. His clothes were relaxed: a white Henley with loose fitting straight white jeans that sag slightly around his hips with a pair of white leather high top Givenchy sneakers.

"You looking good," Kiera said. She stood up to give Eli a hug but seeing Robin approaching caused her hug to be hesitant.

"What's wrong?" Eli asked her with confusion on his face. He looked in the direction Kiera was looking. Eli's face lit up when he saw Robin wearing her white wrap dress and to die for red patent leather pumps. Her copper-colored hair had been straightened and hung past her shoulders. She was looking nice.

"Hey everybody. Hey…Eli." Robin said taking him in from head to toe. "Well, don't you look rather handsome."

"Don't I look good?" Eli joked.

Kiera felt a pang of jealousy. She was Eli's date. Truth be told, she didn't want him talking to Robin's no-good ass. Period. And it sickened her of how Robin was being so fake.

"Yeah, I like it," Robin grinned. She looked at Kiera, "Oh hey. Didn't see you standing there."

Kiera clicked her tongue and rolled her eyes.

Eli told Robin, "Could you excuse me for just one second?"

"Sure," Robin said watching Eli walk away to join his brother and Eric standing off in the distance.

Kiera stood by Robin and said so she could only hear, "You a fake, phony bitch."

Robin looked at wearing a befuddled expression, "What are you talking about?"

"What if I told him about you?"

"Okay, I'm lost. Tell him what?"

"That you're seeing somebody else."

Robin shrugged. She was relieved that that was all Kiera was talking about. "We're not in a monogamous relationship anyway."

"Yeah, but it's who you're seeing. Eli will not appreciate it."

"Now what the hell are you talking about?" Robin asked. She was starting to grow annoyed with Kiera's meddling.

Kiera narrowed her eyes at Robin. "Bitch don't play dumb. You know exactly who I'm talking about."

"You know what? Whatever," Robin said rolling her eyes as she turned to walk away from Kiera.

Kiera wore a satisfied grin. "Yeah. Whatever."

––––––––

The level of sophistication and class represented the ambiance of Southern Wild. It was the perfect venue for such a party. Ivory linen against mahogany seating and flooring. There was wait staff, concierge, a dj, host, and security.

Cesar was thrilled to see Lovely fall into her role as an heiress and millionaire's wife. She was quite the trophy wife especially considering she had a baby just eight weeks earlier. Her black hair had been straightened, and it fell down to her shoulders. The white dress she wore had the back out, a halter front that was cut low, and a snug fitting skirt. The silver strappy platform pumps she wore sparkled along with the platinum and diamond jewels she wore. Lovely looked like money this day. Too bad a woman like her wasn't on his arm although Cesar would prefer it to be Lovely.

At her side was an equally stunning being. Abe strayed from the suited-up look. Abe's big muscular arms were exposed, and women stared at him with their mouths open. He too was drenched in platinum and diamonds. Cesar had to admit that they were quite the superlative couple. *If only,* Cesar thought.

Luciano tapped Cesar on the arm and pointed to the lady that just walked in the door. Cesar looked across the room. It was Sarah with Esau. As usual, she was radiant. She looked ten years younger than her age. Her perfect smile was engaging.

Cesar asked in Italian if Luciano had had a sexual relationship with the woman.

In his careless way of speaking, Luciano said, "It wasn't a relationship. It was an on again off again thing…you know…but…it was right after your mother passed. I wasn't in my right frame of mind."

Cesar chuckled, "That's for sure." Cesar's eyes found Abe in the crowd. "You know he reminds me of a Pavoni."

Luciano smiled when he replied with, "That I know."

Cesar stated, "If I didn't know any better I would think we were blood-related."

Luciano kept his eyes on Abe, admiring the younger man from afar. "What if I told you that I believe I am his father?"

"I wouldn't doubt you," Cesar stated.

"Never doubt me, son," Luciano quipped.

"What about the other two?"

Luciano took a sip of his champagne and said, "I believe they may be my sons also. Not really sure."

Cesar asked, "How will you know for certain if Abe, Ike, and Eli are your sons?"

"I'm almost positive, but Sarah has been making up a lot of lies that I plan to get to the bottom of." Luciano looked across the way and stared at the strikingly good-looking woman. Sarah glanced their way. She held Luciano's gaze for several seconds before turning away.

———

Robin knew her eyes were playing tricks on her. She just knew her lover wasn't at this party. Why didn't he tell her he would be here? She wondered. She saw him talking to a couple of other guys. He was looking very debonair in his all white.

Robin was on her way to him when the sight of Kiera and Eli caught her attention. They were talking about something. It didn't seem as if Kiera was saying anything alarming. Kiera was being watched because she couldn't be trusted.

When Robin returned her attention back to Esau, he was walking away from the two men he had been talking to. He was looking for somebody. *Oh, my God*, Robin thought. *His wife must be here*. Well, the woman didn't know about Robin. Robin caught up with him in the thick sea of white.

"Hey!" she called.

He turned around and was somewhat shocked to see her. "Hey," he said with hesitance.

"I'm surprised to see you here."

"I'm here with my wife," he said remaining indifferent.

"Where is she?"

"That doesn't matter. I don't think it's a good idea that we're seen talking," he said and began to walk away.

"Wait," Robin said resisting the urge to grab him.

"Not here Robin," he said and walked away. Robin stood there looking after him as he disappeared amongst the partiers. Being brushed off like that bruised her feelings. She turned her attention back to Eli. This time he was entertaining someone else. Robin walked in his direction. Not giving the person he was talking to too much thought, Robin interrupted, "Eli, can you dance with me or something?"

Eli frowned then glanced over at the person before him. She just stood there. Eli looked back at Robin, "That was really rude."

"I'm sorry," Robin pouted. She looked at the person to apologize. She was taken aback when she realized the person was a female. At first, Robin thought it was a small framed man. What gave her gender away was the two small bumps poking through her white v-neck tee and the protrusion of her small hips in the white pants she wore. Other than that, the short baby dreads and the make-up-less face alerted Robin she was anything else but a young male.

"You're fine," she said. She looked up at Eli and offered him a small smile. "It was good seeing you. Maybe we can catch up a little before I head back."

Ignoring Robin, Eli said, "You don't have to walk off just yet. It's been a long time since...I've seen you."

Robin asked, "Who is this, Eli? Now, who's being rude? You're not going to introduce us."

Eli rolled his eyes. Frustrated and annoyed, he said dryly, "Robin this is Kris. Kris, this Robin."

Robin plastered a forced smile on her face, "Hi."

"Hey," Kris said softly. She looked at Eli. "I'll call you."

"Please do. And don't leave before coming to see me," Eli said. Robin didn't like the sincerity in Eli's voice. It was almost too close to having feelings for someone. And that was something Eli just didn't show.

Robin wore a look of disdain as she watched Kris walk away. She asked Eli, "How do you know that?"

"That?" Eli asked angrily.

"What is she to you? A cousin or something?"

"Robin, don't start this bullshit," Eli said with aggravation. "Fuck this shit. I need a damn drink."

Robin's mouth hung open with surprise as she watched Eli walk away from her. Really? She thought.

———

Looking at the older men at the round dining table with their elegant wives Abe would have thought he was on the set of a mafia movie. They all sat around chatting in their heavy accents and sipping on expensive champagne and wine. Ahkil, Luciano, Cesar, and Mano.

What Abe never realized was that Mano was Lovely's father's brother. And Ahkil was their uncle. These men were now his business partners. It was a little awkward for Abe knowing what he had done to Pras. However, Abe had to play it cool.

174

Luciano was smiling from ear to ear. "This feels good. What do you say, Abe?"

"I feel fine," Abe smiled back.

"But I'm ready to move forward with the resort and the condos," Luciano said.

Abe was confused. "What condos?"

"The ones I wanna build downtown," Luciano said. His face lit up with excitement. "Abe, we're about to own Nashville. Just be prepared."

"Sounds good to me," Abe said. He looked up and saw Antino with his wife Evelyn heading their way.

"Ah! Here he is," Luciano exclaimed. He stood up to greet Antino and cheek-kissed Evelyn.

Antino looked in Abe's direction and gave him a raised eyebrow smirk. Abe gave a subtle nod. Neither one wanted to elude to the fact that they were familiar with one another already.

"He's been in and out of town, but Abe I'd like you to meet Antino, my brother," Luciano said. "Antino is actually the regional director of our chains on the east coast."

Abe was shocked to learn that Antino was a part of BevyCo too and Luciano's brother. BevyCo derived from their mothers' side of the family. BevyCo was started with their mothers' father Frankie Pavoni. He went into partnership with Bhavesh Prasad who was Lovely's great-grandfather when they went into the casino business. This started the long-standing friendship between the Pavonies and Prasads.

Abe knew that if the others were aware of Antino's scheming ways and underhand doings he along with Abe would be dead.

As the men got rowdy and into the party, Antino took the opportunity to pull Abe aside. The older man smiled at Abe, "How are things, Abe?"

"Fuck that," Abe said keeping his eyes on the rest of the men. He didn't want anybody to hear any of their conversation. Abe said in a low tone, "Tell me what the fuck is going on?"

"Nothing," Antino smirked. "Nothing at all." He looked past Abe at Lovely. "Your wife sure is beautiful."

Through gritted teeth, Abe said, "Don't fuck with me."

"What?" Antino asked playing innocent.

Abe was losing his patience. He shook his head as this situation was becoming more complex. All he knew was he was recruited to do a job. He went through with it. Now he was amongst the people that had strong ties to the people he helped to kill. And Antino was the link to them all.

Antino said in a comforting way, "Look, you don't know nothing. Keep doing what you've been doing. In the meantime, come over for drinks and catch up one on one. It's been a while."

"It's been a while for a reason," Abe said. Abe knew Antino and how sheisty he could be. He worked up under him for almost ten years. Antino was always up to something looking for his next big heist and getting over on people. Abe agreed to meet for drinks later that week before excusing himself to grab Lovely

————

It wasn't surprising to Ike that Tomiko would abandon him during the party. If she hadn't, he would think something was terribly wrong with her.

Seeing Melissa alone at an almost vacant table, Ike made his way over to her. "Where's Reggie?"

Melissa kept her eyes on the crowd before her. "He's somewhere out there."

Ike took in Melissa's beauty and smiled. "You look really nice tonight."

Melissa didn't respond.

"So, what is this Melissa?" Ike asked with impatience.

She looked up at him for the first time. "Nothing Ike. I'm just sitting at this table sipping on my drink and watching people dance."

"I'm talking about us," he said taking a seat next to her.

"We're fine," she said curtly.

"We are? You haven't been really talking to me lately," Ike said.

"I've been busy."

Ike looked out into the crowd in search for his wife. She wasn't hard to find since she was wearing a very wide red belt to accentuate her waist in the already fitted white dress she was wearing.

Ike scoffed with a shake of his head. Seeing her talking so close to Reggie was what Ike actually expected to see. He said to Melissa, "Do you wanna know who my wife is fucking?"

"No," Melissa answered quickly.

"I think you should know," Ike said. He pointed over to where Tomiko and Reggie were enjoying each other's company. "You see those two—"

"I already know Ike," Melissa stated.

Ike was confused. "Already know what?"

Melissa looked at him with eyes filling with hurt and tears, "I know. You don't have to say it. But right now, I don't wanna think about it. I just wanna enjoy this party."

Ike wasn't sure of what to say. What exactly did Melissa know? He had to hear her say it.

When he opened his mouth to say something else, seeing another unlikely pair speaking threw Ike off. He knew that Cesar probably wasn't aware of who Lorenzo was so Cesar would get a pass, for now; however, there was something about Cesar that wasn't sitting well with Ike as of late. But right at the moment, Cesar wasn't as big of an issue as Lorenzo's presence at this party. Abe wasn't going to be happy at all.

———————

Seeing Kris at the party was a real surprise for Eli. When his eyes landed on her, it instantly made him tingle. Feelings quickly surfaced, and Eli realized how much he missed Kris. He was disappointed that she had to leave so soon and that she would only be in town for a few days.

"Come here Eli," Kiera called out to him disrupting him from his thoughts. She opened her arms wide to him. "You look sad. You need a hug?"

Smelling the liquor from where he stood, Eli said, "Your ass is drunker than a mothafucka."

"No," Kiera shook her head from side to side. "I am not drunk."

"Yes, you are," Eli chuckled as Kiera wrapped her arms around him.

Kiera snuggled close to his chest and inhaled his cologne. "I love you, Eli. And you smell so good!"

"Get off of me," he said trying to pry her arms away. She held onto him tighter.

"Don't do that," Kiera mumbled. "You making me dizzy."

"If you throw up on me, I will smack you," he told her. Eli looked down at Kiera to find that her eyes were closed, and she was wearing a smile. He asked aloud, "Is this broad going to sleep on me standing up?"

"Oh, how cute," Aisha said as she approached Eli and Kiera.

"Why are you here?" Eli asked with disgust etched across his face.

"To have a good time like everybody else," Aisha said with a smug smile.

Eli eyed her from head to toe. She wasn't as polished as she used to be when she was dating Abe. This gave Eli great pleasure. "Aisha, are you getting fat?"

"Are you still gay?" Aisha shot back.

"Do you still swallow sperm?" Eli retorted.

"I bet you swallow more than I have."

Kiera released Eli and looked at Aisha, "Bitch bye 'fore I snatch that weave outcho head and reveal them bald ass edges."

Eli pretended to be sympathetic, "Ah! You got bald edges. Next time instead of swallowing, have them skeet that shit around your hairline. Protein is good for hair growth."

Aisha stood there looking at both of them with disgust. "Whatever bitches."

In the distance, the sight of Abe and Lovely caught Aisha's attention. Eli followed her gaze. "Don't they look so nice? You wish it was you, don't you Aisha?"

Aisha rolled her eyes with a dismissive attitude and walked away.

"I can't stand her," Eli murmured. He looked over at Kiera who seemed to be swaying back and forward. "You need to take your ass somewhere and sit down!"

"I'm alright. Can you go get me another drink?"

Eli grabbed Kiera by the arm and led her to an empty table. He sat her down in one of the chairs. "Have a seat. Don't move. Stay here until I come back for you."

"What about that drink though?"

Eli was about to respond until he felt someone touch the back of his shoulder.

"Eli sweetie, can you get your mother an apple martini from the bar," Sarah asked as she took a seat beside Kiera whose head was on the table now. "Is she alright?"

"No. She's drunk. Are you too?"

"No. Why would you ask me that?"

"Cause you crazy in hell if you think I'm about to fetch you a drink."

Sarah narrowed her eyes at Eli. "Son, do as I ask."

"Mama, why are you even here? You're not young anymore. You should be in Kentucky somewhere playing bingo."

"I am young. You see your aunt Mary out there? She's older than I am. And look at her friend Lois Jean. She keeping up with the young ones out there," Sarah laughed.

"And she need to sit down too."

"Stop being a hater, Eli," Sarah said playfully.

Eli looked out at the dance floor to locate the two older ladies dancing. He shook his head at the hilarity of them trying to imitate the latest dances. "Mama, what the hell Lois Jean got on? She should never ever wear that again. And somebody need to give her some Zoloft cause them titties is just sad."

Sarah burst out in a fit of laughter. "Stop that Eli!"

Robin made her way over to the table but didn't sit down. "Hi, Mrs. Masters."

"Hello young lady," Sarah responded looking Robin over.

Robin tapped Eli, "Can I talk to you?"

"About what?" Eli asked. He had a feeling it wouldn't be a conversation he would enjoy.

Sarah interrupted, "Oh Eli! There's your daddy. Can you tell him where I am when you go to get my drink? Please?"

"Your daddy is here?" Robin asked Eli. "I've never seen or met him before."

"That's because he's an asshole and don't come around much," Sarah said.

Eli sighed. These women were wearing him out. He reluctantly went to the bar to get Sarah's drink. On his way back, he told Esau he was wanted over at the table.

"What is it now woman?" Esau was asking as he approached the table.

"Nothing. I just wanted you to know where I was," Sarah said sipping on her drink.

Esau shook his head. Robin standing off to the side caught his attention, and he stared at her. Sarah took notice and said, "Oh Esau, that's Robin, Eli's friend. Robin, this is Eli's daddy Esau."

Robin just stared at Esau.

Esau said, "Nice to meet you, young lady."

Robin nodded. She turned to Eli. "Give me a call whenever you can. I think I need to be heading out of here."

"Okay," Eli said to Robin's back as she hurried away. That was weird, Eli thought. He was curious to know why Robin reacted like that.

———

Melissa was tired of wondering, so she bluntly asked Jackie, "What's going on between you and Ike?"

"Absolutely nothing," Jackie willingly answered. She was thinking it was time to give up on Ike and invest her energy and time elsewhere.

"Y'all seem to be really friendly," Melissa commented.

"Yeah, cause that's all that we are; friends. Don't get me wrong, I find Ike irresistibly handsome and I have somewhat of a crush on him, but I guess going beyond friendship is not in the cards."

"That's good to know," Melissa said under her breath.

"Why is that?" Jackie asked.

"Well you know me and him had something going on," Melissa stated as she watched Ike talk amongst a group of men. "We've backed off a little, but the feelings are there. So, if you don't mind...give him some breathing room."

Jackie was appalled by what Melissa had told her. Why would she even reveal her secret like that? To save her relationship with Ike?

Jackie asked, "But aren't you married?"

"So is Ike."

"He'll be a divorced man in a few months."

"What does that have to do with what I said?"

"Your husband is only a few feet away, and you're telling another woman who is single to stay away from a man that's about to be divorced. I'm missing something," Jackie said with cynicism.

"What I'm saying to you is don't try to pursue anything with Ike."

"First of all, you can't intimidate me. Secondly, all you should be concerned with is telling his son the truth about who he is. If the next time I'm at Ike's, and Mekhi is there, I'm telling him."

Melissa slung her drink in Jackie's face which shocked everyone close by. Ike saw it and walked over to the commotion. Melissa was saying, "Bitch don't fuck with me and mine! You worry about yours, you broke ass Jill Scott wannabe."

Jackie was still in shock that Melissa would do such a thing. Ike tried to help pat her dry as he asked, "What happened?"

"We exchange some words about you. I said something she didn't like and then this happened," Jackie said. Her eyes got teary eyed. She removed her glasses to wipe them clean. Reggie had pulled Melissa off to the side and was talking to her.

"What did you say, Jackie?" Ike wanted to know as Tomiko approached them.

"I told her she needed to be truthful about her son," Jackie answered. She dabbed at her dress. When Tomiko arrived at Ike's side, she just stared at her.

Tomiko wore a humored smirk. "Looks like your dress is ruined."

Ike shot Tomiko a look.

"I'm just gonna get Robin to take me home and get this dress off of me," Jackie said.

"Robin left already," Ike said. He looked over at Tomiko, "Could you take her home since you were about to leave anyway?"

"But I'm not going that way," Tomiko answered. Without a care in the world, Tomiko called over her shoulder as she walked away, "See you later Ike."

Jackie shook her head with pity. Both Tomiko and Melissa were crazy.

"You know what? I've been here long enough. How about I take you home after I speak to my brother," Ike suggested.

Jackie nodded. It made sense to just leave.

Lovely felt like she was walking on cloud nine. She hadn't felt so overjoyed ever in her adulthood. She felt great. She knew from the steady flow of compliments she looked great. Abe couldn't keep his hands off of her. But she thought he had too much to drink. She had to tear away from him just now because she thought he would have sex with her right there in the middle of the dance floor.

"Your ass is sexy, you know that?" Abe whispered in her ear.

"Will you stop that?" Lovely giggled.

"When we get home I'ma tear this pussy up."

Lovely blushed with embarrassment.

Abe was tickled. "Why do you do that? You turn so red."

"Is it possible for me to turn red?"

"You do all the time. It's cute."

"Abe, you're drunk," Lovely giggled.

"So!"

Lovely laughed. She wrapped her arms around him tightly. "Baby, I want us to be like this forever."

"You want us to forever be dancing?"

"No silly. I mean like this. The way we are with each other."

"In love?"

"Yes!"

"We will be. Forever and ever...and ever."

"Oh my gosh, your ass is so silly when you drink."

"I'm not drunk with liquor though. I'm drunk with you!"

Lovely giggled again. She said, "I gotta pee."

"C'mon, let's go."

"No, I'm fine. I can go on my own."

"You sure?"

"Yeah. I got this."

"Don't be too long baby. I forget how to breathe without you near," Abe said reluctant to let Lovely go. He watched her as she carefully headed towards the second-tier level where there was a private restroom. *Damn, she was fine*, Abe thought with a smile on his face.

A tap on his shoulder snapped him out of lusting over his wife. He turned around to face Kenya. She smiled up at him, "Hi stranger."

"Hey," he said. He was still wearing the smile Lovely had left him with.

"You seem to be really happy," Kenya noted.

"I am."

"Mmm hmm," Kenya said nonchalantly. She nodded in the direction Lovely went. "So, I see you two are making things work."

"That's the love of my life," Abe beamed.

The slighted look on Kenya's face expressed she didn't like what Abe said. Regardless if Abe was with someone else, Kenya had always been regarded as the love of Abe's life. Kenya was just waiting for Abe to come to his senses. She said, "Is this love of your life okay with you killing her parents? Have y'all gotten past those issues?"

Abe's smile faded.

Seeing the scorn across Abe's face Kenya added sarcastically, "Oh yeah. That's right. She doesn't know. Sure would be a shame if she did."

With his attention on his oldest brother approaching him, Abe shook his head pitying her. He lightly chuckled, "I really wanted to like you and think of you as a cool person Kenya. I never thought the day would come that I would think better of your sister than I do of you."

"Who? Kiera? That girl is still grimy. Trust and believe that."

Coldly Abe said, "Yeah, but she knows her mothafuckin place. Know yours and get the fuck out of my face."

Ike looked from an appalled Kenya to Abe, "Sorry to interrupt but I gotta talk to you before I leave Abe."

"Sure," Abe said giving Kenya one last glance. He reminded her before walking off, "Know your place."

Once she was finished with her business in the lady's room, Lovely walked out oblivious to her company. She concentrated on getting back to her horny husband. He wanted to feel inside her so bad. She told Abe he had to wait...but then again...tonight had her feeling some kind of way too.

"Hey, pretty lady."

Lovely's head jerked in the direction of the voice. It sounded very familiar.

"It's me. Lorenzo. Remember?"

"Oh," Lovely said. She immediately felt apprehensive because she remembered how Abe reacted when Lorenzo showed up at the house. And then there was his voice. Lovely hated it. "I didn't realize you would be here Lorenzo."

"Yeah well you know I'm fam'ly."

"Yeah." Although Lovely didn't feel comfortable, she didn't want to alert anyone and cause a scene.

Lorenzo said, "You know Lovely is a nice name. It's different. Looking at you though you coulda been named Pretty or Beautiful but Lovely fits you nice."

Lovely continued to walk. "Thanks."

Lorenzo walked with her. "I seen you out there dancing with Abe. You move good."

Lovely offered an uneasy smile, "Thanks."

Lorenzo eyed the chunky diamond platinum ring on her left ring finger. That ring had to be six figures. With a woman like Lovely, he'd put a rock on her hand like that too.

"I see you and Abe got married," he mentioned.

"Oh yeah, we did," Lovely said, her right hand went to cover her wedding ring.

"I didn't even know Abe had gotten married. Nobody told me nothing," Lorenzo lied.

"Are you and Abe close?" Lovely asked knowing the truth behind this question already.

"We kinda go way back. He's like a brother to me."

"I'm surprised I hadn't met you sooner then."

"I travel a lot and rarely stay still long enough to come around. But I'm glad to see he's married and settled down. Especially with a woman like you."

Lovely smiled awkwardly. "Well, any family of Abe's is family of mine."

Lorenzo eyes went to the deep plunge of Lovely's dress. The swells of her breasts were enticing. "Well family, can I get a hug?"

Before Lovely could object, she felt Lorenzo grabbing her to pull her in for a hug. She resisted, but she felt his hand grab her around the back and groped her ass. She pushed him away. "Don't you ever touch me like that again!"

Lorenzo said soothingly, "I didn't mean no harm mama. Calm down."

Lovely began to look around in a panic. Her comfort and security level dropped. All of the white before her was a big blur. The space around her seemed to be closing in.

———

The rage manifesting in Abe was inevitable. He didn't know what made him angrier: the fact that this mothafucka was there and with his wife or the terrified look on Lovely's face.

"Abe?" Ike questioned. He had been talking to Abe about seeing Lorenzo at the party when suddenly Abe stopped talking, and something in the distance caught his attention.

From the expression on Abe's face, Luciano could tell whatever Abe was looking at wasn't a good thing. Luciano turned in the direction Abe was looking. "Who is that with Lovely?"

Eli's head whipped around to get a look. "Oh shit!" Before he knew it, Abe was charging in Lovely's and Lorenzo's direction. "Lu, it's about to be some smoke in the city!"

Luciano gestured to his men to follow behind him as he trailed behind Abe and Eli.

"Hey Abe," Lorenzo smirked. "I was just keeping your beautiful wife here company."

Abe grabbed Lovely as she was talking, "Baby, listen. Don't be getting—" She was interrupted by Abe pushing her aside.

Eli was there to prevent her from losing her balance. "Are you okay?

Lovely was vexed. "I'm fine."

In defense mode and ready to pounce, Abe said to Lorenzo, "Why are you here?"

Lorenzo looked around the club with a smug expression. "I'm here like everyone else. I'm here to enjoy this lovely party."

Abe glanced around questioning, "Who the fuck invited him here?"

Lorenzo stood there wearing the most annoying smirk on his face. It enraged Abe even more.

"You stay the fuck away from my wife," Abe said coldly. "I already done told your ass once."

"Or what?" Lorenzo asked.

"You think I'm mothafuckin playing!" Abe's fist formed at his side.

Lorenzo looked down at Abe's fist and at Abe's clenched jaw. "I'm not here to start any mess, Abe. Like I said, I'm just here to enjoy this party. Your wife ain't got nothing to do with why I'm here. I'm actually here to see you. You know...about that payment."

Antino walked up behind Lorenzo wearing a displeased frown. "Lorenzo! Stop with the nonsense."

"I'm not doing nothing but tryna have a *lovely* time," Lorenzo smirked.

Antino tried to get Lorenzo to stop with the innuendo, but it was too late. Abe was already ticked off that Lorenzo was there.

Before anyone knew it or could stop it, Abe pounced Lorenzo and chaos broke out. Lovely cried out for Abe to stop hitting his cousin while about four or five guys tried to get Abe off of Lorenzo. His mother, Esau, and Aunt Mary rushed over as well as others to see what the commotion was about.

"Get him the fuck outta here!" Abe demanded as Eric and Ike pulled him back. Abe spat, "Didn't I tell your bitch ass to stay the fuck away! Why you wanna fuck with me!"

Lovely pushed him. "Abe, stop!" As a reaction, Abe pushed Lovely back. She was shocked. "Really Abe?"

As she was doing that Lorenzo took the opportunity to swing on Abe. It didn't connect, but it pissed Abe off even more. Lovely hopped in front of him.

"Get out the got-damn way Lovely!" Abe barked and pulled her so hard by her arm it sent her spinning out of control. Eli had to catch her. Lovely was beyond horrified and pissed at the same time.

Abe pounced on Lorenzo until they were pulled apart. Not being able to get to Lorenzo like he wanted, Abe was able to realize what he had done to Lovely. "Baby I'm so sorry."

Lovely pushed Abe as hard as she could, but he barely budged. She was angry. "I ain't with this violence Abe! So, stop...," she pushed him again, "...it. Stop it!"

"Stop Lovely," he said in a calmer voice. "You're gonna hurt yourself."

"So, the way you just jerked me in this stupid rage of yours didn't almost just hurt me?" Lovely was seething. She cut her eyes at him as she turned away from him and stormed away.

Lorenzo was helped to his feet. He was bleeding from his mouth. He was checking his teeth to make sure all of his teeth were still intact. He started laughing maniacally. He called out, "I still love you cousin! We can make up tomorrow...Bring Lovely."

Why did he say that? Before Abe could get to him Tommy and Vic, the de Rosa's security was grabbing Lorenzo up and dragging him towards the door. He tried to give them a fight, but he gave up and cooperated. Antino's men Travis and Carter helped to calm Lorenzo down as their crew exited the club.

———————

Back in the private office those closest to Abe was trying to calm him down and remind him everyone was there to have a good time and celebrate this special day.

"Abe, you've upset Lovely," Sarah fussed. She grabbed his face and turned it toward a teary eye Lovely. "See. Look at her."

Abe was shocked that his mother was even touching him. In astonishment, he stared at Sarah.

Esau side-eyed Sarah and tugged her away. "Don't go getting in the middle of his problems!"

Sarah jerked away from Esau. "You don't tell me what to do."

"See that's where that hot-headedness come from. You!" Esau shot.

Ike frowned, "Don't be talking to Mama like that!"

"Boy, you have really gotten besides yourself. All of you have. Now I'm getting real sick of you talking to me like you gon do something! I am your daddy, and I will lay your ass out!"

Sarah and Eli both had to hold Ike back. Sarah said, "Ike! Do not disrespect your father."

Ike sneered. "Fuck Esau!"

Sarah slapped Ike's chest. "You stop that!"

"So, you wanna side with the devil now Ike?" Esau taunted.

"Let it go, Esau," Sarah said.

"Naw, let his dumb ass talk," Ike said angrily. He glared at Esau and said, "I ain't never liked you. Abe should feel lucky that he doesn't have you for an actual father."

Esau exclaimed, "I'm glad I'm not! He's the fuckin' devil!"

"The only devil I've ever saw when we were kids was you!" Ike retorted.

Sarah shook her head desperately at Ike begging him to be quiet. Esau let out a maniacal and taunting laugh.

Abe went to Lovely and hugged her to him. "I'm sorry."

Lovely wrapped her arms around him tightly listening to the mayhem about to start.

Sarah said to Esau, "I thought we were back here to calm Abe down from beating the mess out of your nephew!"

Esau's expression filled with disgust as Luciano and Cesar with their security came into the room. "These mothafuckas," he said under his breath.

Sarah shot Esau a look and asked, "What did you say?"

"I wasn't talking to you," Esau said smartly in a raised voice.

"Watch your tone dude," Abe said. Lovely clutched Abe's shirt as if she could actually stop him from attacking someone.

Esau spat, "Fuck you. You are not to speak to me directly. Or have you forgotten?"

Luciano spoke, "Speaking to him like that will not be necessary."

"I speak to him any kind of way I want," Esau countered. "Furthermore, whatchu got to do with it?"

The two men stared the other down, neither showing signs of backing down.

Esau scoffed arrogantly, "That's what I thought."

Luciano grabbed the remote sitting on the desk and threw it forcefully at Esau's face and was upon him connecting a punch to his jaw, so fast Esau didn't have enough time to react. Nobody saw that coming. Luciano said, "*È Cagna! Ti ucciderò e ti nutrire i cani che scopano!*"

Cesar wasn't surprised. Luciano turned to Tommy and Vic angrily, "You 'posed to see that coming and punch him for me, no! I pay you for nothing!" He started ranting in Italian.

Cesar pulled Luciano behind him before Esau tried to retaliate. Tommy and Vic were already there to escort Esau out.

Even Sarah was too stunned to come to Esau's aide. David, who had been there during the whole thing advised Esau to walk out of the room with him.

Antino made his presence known by stepping fully into the room. He looked at Abe with concern in his eyes. "Are you alright son?"

"I'm fine," Abe mumbled angrily.

Luciano looked at his brother then back at Sarah. He stared at Abe. His eyes shifted back to Antino then to Sarah again. Was it possible that Antino was Abe's real father and not him? As if he was hit with an epiphany Luciano said, "Now I understand why you wanted everything to stay a secret. You said you were raped. You weren't raped. It was Antino...So all this time you were sleeping with both of us?"

The room became silent. Sarah looked over at Antino then at Abe. She looked at Luciano, "Are you serious Lu?"

Luciano was becoming infuriated, "Sarah, I'm very serious."

"Is this true?" Abe asked. He was confused but anxious to know and understand what Luciano was talking about.

"Tell him, Sarah," Luciano demanded.

"How did this become about me?" Sarah asked about to come undone.

"You're a liar. You're manipulative. You're cunning. Vindictive. Sneaky." Antino said narrowing his eyes at her.

Sarah looked at Abe and in a flippant manner said, "Okay. I'm sorry. Luciano or Antino might be your father. There. I said it. Do whatchu want with that; I'm gone." Sarah turned to leave.

Antino grabbed Sarah by the arm. "Nuh-uh." He turned her to face Abe. "Tell him the truth."

"You've already laid it out there," Sarah snapped. She pulled away from Antino.

"You tell him the truth," Antino exclaimed.

Sarah showed only irritation, no remorse. She groaned. She looked at Abe blankly. "I was never raped with you. I got pregnant with you after I slept with Antino. I made the rape thing up to cover up my wrongdoings. Sorry."

"What?" Abe asked in disbelief. "What? So, all my life you treated me like shit, named me that fucked up name, never loved me as a mother should and let Esau beat me on a regular basis because you were a hoe!"

Lovely tried to hold onto Abe, but he was getting worked up all over again. Abe asked, "Why! Why would you do that?"

"I don't know," Sarah said as her voice trailed to a whisper. She finally began to show guilt and remorse. Tears filled her eyes. She reached out to him, "I'm sorry."

Abe punched the wall leaving a nice size hole behind. "Do you know what I became—The things I've done? All because of your fucking lies!"

"I'm sorry Abe," Sarah cried.

"Don't touch me!" Abe pushed Sarah away from him as he brushed past her.

Eli looked at Sarah and thought how pitiful she was. He turned away to leave.

Sarah called out, "Eli, I'm sorry...Ike...I'm sorry..."

Ike glared at her as he was just as disgusted. He followed his brothers out of the room. This night wouldn't end on a good note.

Chapter Thirteen

L ovely wanted to comfort Abe, but he wouldn't let her. He had become distant. He didn't even talk to her on the way home. It was extremely late, and she was tired. Her feet hurt, and her body ached in certain places. She couldn't believe what had transpired that night, but at least Abe knew the truth.

"Abe," she spoke softly. She had come out of her closet dressed for bed. Abe sat in the sitting area of the bedroom in complete silence. Lovely called out his name again, "Abe?"

"What Lovely?" he snapped.

"Baby are you okay?"

"No, I'm not. And you know I'm not." His voice held irritation and frustration.

Lovely sat down beside him. She understood his current state. She didn't want to pressure him, but she didn't want to abandon him when he was in such need. "Abe, I know—"

"Will you stop saying my damn name!"

Lovely was offended that he raised his voice at her. She wasn't used to that. Abe never talked to her in the way that he was just now. Lovely got up and left Abe with his own thoughts and feelings. She got in the bed but knew she wouldn't be able to sleep. Abe got up from the sofa and left out of the room. Lovely was tempted to go after him but she wouldn't.

Lovely awakened at dawn for one of her many trips to the bathroom to discover Abe hadn't returned. He hadn't been in bed all night. After she handled her business in the bathroom, she went looking for him. She went all over the house, and that was a workout. She went to the garage to discover an empty space where Abe's Aston Martin should have been.

Lovely hurried back to her bedroom and retrieved her phone. "Call Abe," she said to it. The call went directly to his voicemail. She called again. Voicemail. She pressed the button on the digital alarm on the nightstand. It read out the time was 5:42 am. Where the hell was Abe?

————

Robin couldn't believe any of this. She paced the floor of the condo waiting for her lover or Esau or whatever his name was to show up. She had text him several times. He had to be aware that she was at the condo.

The doorknob turning halted Robin. She stood in the middle of the living room space waiting for him to enter through the door.

Esau walked in locking his gaze on her. Robin was glaring at him. He didn't say anything as he locked the door behind him. He walked towards Robin still not saying anything. When he reached out to touch her, Robin took a step back.

"I didn't know Robin," Esau said.

"You told me to just call you E!" Robin snapped.

"Yeah and I told you to call me that just to be on the safe side," he explained.

"The safe side? What did you think I would do? Look you up and stalk you at your house or something?" Robin asked angrily.

Esau shrugged. "I don't know. It has happened before."

"Before? So, you always cheat on your wife?"

"I have cheated before but why would you care?"

"Normally I wouldn't. But you're Eli's daddy. I know your wife!"

"So, what? It changes nothing between us," he said cupping her face between his hands. He kissed her on the lips. "I love you, Robin."

Robin noticed the purple bruise on Esau's face. "What happened? Who hit you?"

Esau turned away from her and went into the kitchen. "Lu and I got into it."

"Does Lu's face look as bad as yours?" Robin asked.

Esau removed a wine bottle from the wine rack. "I don't wanna talk about that. The whole night was fucked up. I just wanna relax and unwind."

"I've been fucking Eli," Robin blurted out.

Esau stopped what he was doing. "You what?"

"Eli is the friend," Robin said.

"My son? You've been fucking my son?" Esau asked growing irate.

"Yes. But E, I didn't know he was your son. Had you told me your real name then maybe I would have put two and two together."

"Well, how about you just keep your goddamn legs closed!"

Robin snapped, "You can't get mad at me!"

Esau stood there with a faraway look in his eyes.

"Baby, you can't get mad," Robin said in a calmer tone.

"You're right. But if I find out you're still fucking him after today, I will beat your ass."

———

Abe walked into Antino's hearthroom impressed with the décor although it was something he wouldn't do in his own home. Antino had turned this room into his redneck-I-went-hunting-and-brought-everything-I-killed-back room. Abe laughed inwardly, but Antino had it set up in such a way that looked good, classy, and not so hillbilly-ish. The polar bearskin rug was creepy because the head was still attached. Abe made sure he sat at the tail end of the rug.

Abe kept his eyes on Antino the entire time Antino made his way over to where Abe sat. Antino chuckled. "You don't like the rug, Abe?"

"It just look...dead," Abe said.

"That's what it is," Antino laughed.

"Why you got all this dead shit in here. PETA would come up in here and whoop the shit outcho ass," Abe joked.

"PETA would have a nice spot up there between those two wolf heads too," Antino countered with a laugh.

Antino ordered for his henchmen to stay outside the double doors to the hearthroom. Antino wore an amused grin. "Well, well, well. It's been a while since I've been graced by your presence. To what do I owe the pleasure of this lovely little meeting?"

"I'ma cut to the chase. You know why I'm here." Abe asked, "How long have you known?"

"I guess I always kinda knew when you first came to me," he answered.

Abe said nothing. He didn't want his anger to explode. Antino knew Abe could possibly had been his son the whole time and yet Antino had Abe in the streets breaking every law there was. "You knew all this time?"

"Yeah, I knew. I didn't need Sarah to tell me either although I know there was a great possibility that you could be Lu's son. Hell, you coulda been anybody's son. No offense."

It was hard for Abe to be completely mad. He had to admit that when Antino took him in at age fourteen, he was good to him. He took care of Abe. He fed him and clothed him. He showed him a love he never got being raised by Sarah and Esau. Any other treatment would have been better than what he endured in Sarah and Esau's household. It was what caused him to drop out of school and run away, to begin with. Antino was right there to take Abe in.

"You don't have blue eyes," Abe said.

"No, but me and Lu's mama have them," Antino explained. "She's back in the old country."

"A blue-eyed Italian?"

"Her mama was White. But you. You are a true Pavoni."

"Pavoni?"

"*Pavoni è la famiglia di mia madre.*"

"English, please. So why didn't either of you claim me?"

"The Mancusos had a problem with interracial relationships let alone a biracial child," he said.

Abe gave him a skeptical look. "Was that the real reason for real?"

"It was part of it. The other part was I wanted to leave well enough alone. I simply didn't want to deal with Sarah and Esau. Besides she didn't want her marriage compromised."

Antino studied Abe's face. He looked tired and worn. His eyes were red and puffy from crying. "Abe are you okay?"

Abe ignored the question. He asked instead, "What's up with Lorenzo?"

"What are you talking about?" Antino asked innocently. This was the third time Lorenzo had been brought up as trouble. Frankly, Antino was tired of it.

"Don't play stupid Ant," Abe said. "I know Lorenzo is under you. He doesn't have much sense to be on his own."

"All I know is that he owes money. I can't help him," Antino said.

"How much does he owe?"

Antino shrugged. "I'm not sure."

Abe's eyebrows furrowed. Antino smiled softly up at Abe as if he was admiring him. Antino saw his younger self in Abe from his looks to his mannerisms. Anyone looking at the two could see that it was obvious that they were related in some way.

"He asked for two hundred fifty thousand dollars," Abe said.

"He needs more than that."

"Well, I ain't giving him shit."

"I wouldn't either," Antino said. Out of curiosity, Antino asked, "Why does he feel he can get that much from you?"

"He's trying to blackmail me," Abe said. Despair had replaced the angered expression he was wearing.

"Are you still running from your past and pretending that you once weren't who you were Fyah?"

Abe gave Antino a stern look. "It's in my past and has nothing to do with my present or my future. I just want my family to be safe at this point."

"What about your safety?" Antino posed.

"What about it?"

"That girl. Lovely. Her uncles Ahkil and Mano are still around. What do you think they would do if word got to him that you had something to do with killing their nephew and brother and stealing the money?" Antino smirked as he sipped his drink.

Calmly Abe said, "I'm not worried about them right now. I'm more concerned with Lovely. And let me find out that you're putting Lorenzo up to this. Everybody keeps bringing up Fyah. I will bring him out if need be."

"I know you will. I'm simply forewarning you. Don't be stupid. See Abe you've got all good boy on us and mentoring the youth and going to the church. You've become too relaxed. You need to keep your ear to the streets son."

"Don't call me that."

Antino grinned, "But you are my son even if the DNA says you're not."

"I'm no one's son."

Antino said, "Look. We can discuss that another day. A word from the wise. Keep your eyes and ears open. Everything ain't what it seems. Everyone isn't who they portray to be."

———

Abe walked into the kitchen and was immediately attacked by Aunt Livy and Lulu.

"And where have you been?" Aunt Livy asked. "You had Lovely worried about you."

"Lovely very upset," Lulu said.

Abe looked over to the oversized u-shaped sectional where Lovely was sitting. She was watching him while trying to mask the apprehension. Abe felt bad that he had snapped on her the way he did the night before. He felt like an ass. How could he hurt Lovely like that? She had only been trying to comfort him. Wasn't that what he had vowed to do for her? If it wasn't for him, she wouldn't be in a position where she felt like she needed to help. He regretted staying away from home as well. He had been blessed with too much from Lovely to even act like he would leave her.

"Hey Abe," Kiera called out as he made his way over to Lovely.

"Where you been?" Eli asked. He could tell his brother was going through something heavy. It was evident Abe had been crying. He still had on the clothes he wore to the party, and they were disheveled.

"Taking care of something," Abe mumbled as he knelt down before Lovely. He spoke to her softly. "Lovely, I'm sorry. I didn't mean to treat you like that."

Eli said, "Lovely, don't put up with his bullshit. He already done pulled that shit once. He trying you."

Eli wasn't fast enough to duck the toss pillow Abe slung at him. "Shut'cho ass up."

"I wouldn't forgive your ass," Eli continued as he giggled. "Your ass slung the shit out of poor Lovely. I didn't think her ass would ever stop spinning."

Lovely was laughing. Abe was glad she was able to look past his moodiness and still remain in good spirits. Lovely got up and said to Abe, "C'mon. Let's have a talk."

Abe followed Lovely to their bedroom. She didn't bother sitting, so Abe didn't bother sitting.

Lovely asked, "Where were you and why weren't you answering your phone?"

"I had to clear my head. I just needed that time for myself."

"But I was worried, Abe. You can't keep running and staying away from home when shit gets rough."

"And I'm sorry."

"Another thing. Your behavior yesterday was not cool."

Abe expected that from Lovely. He had no response.

"What is wrong Abe? You've never shown me that side of you. You've never snapped on me before, and then...then you just stay away like I'm gonna be okay with it all!"

"It wasn't personal Lovely. I would never want to hurt you intentionally baby. It's just...well, you know how I felt about my mama and not knowing who my real father was. That's where I went to this morning. I had to talk to Antino."

"What about overnight? Where were you?"

"I was at the office."

"You coulda called me Abe. Not only that we coulda talked last night. I'm your partner. I'm your wife now or have you forgotten that we exchanged vows the first day of this year? Isn't that what I'm supposed to do? I'm supposed to be here for you."

"I know."

"You know? Then let me do it. I don't stop you from being my husband or my friend," she pointed out.

Abe smiled at Lovely's small frame with her hands on her hips. "Come here Lovely."

Lovely stood firm where she was. "No."

He sighed and headed to the bed. He sat down and reached out for her. "Come here, woman."

"You just wanna distract me by getting all mushy and stuff. I'm not falling for it."

"I love you," he said melodiously.

Lovely couldn't resist. She walked over to him. Abe pulled her into his arms. "I promise I will never stay away from home again unless it's for business."

"What about your outbursts?"

"I'll work on it."

Lovely grinned. "I guess I'll accept your apologies…this time."

"It won't happen again," Abe assured her as his phone began ringing. He pulled it from his pocket and looked at the screen. It was Luciano. He answered, "Hello?"

"Hey Abe," Luciano greeted cheerfully.

Abe found himself being hurt the most by Luciano. He felt betrayed by him. Why didn't he share that bit of news with Abe earlier? They had grown really close over the past ten months. Abe just expected more from Luciano, especially after witnessing his commendable work ethics. But work and personal life were two different things.

"Hey," Abe solemnly answered.

"I uh…I just wanted to say that I'm sorry for how that played out yesterday," Luciano said. When Abe didn't respond Luciano continued, "I never knew about you until I met you Thanksgiving. It was then that I confronted Sarah. She insisted that I was not your father. It saddens me to know that I may not be your father after all."

"Why didn't you tell me?" Abe asked. He became irate within seconds. "You know my hurt and frustrations over that matter. You've listened to me talk about it. How come you never said anything?"

"Because she asked me to leave it alone. I almost believed her that she was raped and didn't know who your father was, but you are Pavoni. I've seen you in action. I see how your mind work."

"But I could easily be Antino's child," he said. Lovely gently caressed his back as he talked.

"You could. So that's why I want us to be tested as soon as possible. You, me, Antino, Ike, and Eli."

"Ike and Eli?"

"They may be one of ours too."

Abe shook his head. His mother had created a mess. The two men talked a few minutes more before ending the call.

"Soooo...how are y'all gonna handle this?" Lovely asked.

"I guess we take a DNA test," Abe said as his mind wandered. He got up and pulled Lovely along with him as he headed out of the room.

When Abe entered the family room, Eli asked, "What's wrong with you?"

"Lu wants to test you and Ike too," Abe said.

"Me?" Eli was confused and shocked.

"Yeah."

Eli looked at his arm for emphasis, "I'm too dark to be his child. And my hair ain't like yours. I ain't got no funny looking eyes either."

"None of that matters when it comes to genetics," Abe said.

Kiera, who had been there with Eli asked, "So there's a possibility you might not be Esau's son?"

"I guess," Eli said. "But we shall see."

Chapter Fourteen

Aisha grimaced at the sight of Lorenzo's lip. "He got you pretty good, huh?"

"That's alright. I got something for his ass," Lorenzo mumbled.

"So, what happened?"

"Abe was on some bullshit," Lorenzo said. He tried to focus on the game on television.

"I've never seen Abe be violent," Aisha said with thought. She said, "That's weird."

"You never met the real Abe."

"Who is the real Abe?" she asked.

"A nigga worse than me."

"How worse can you be?"

"What's up with all these questions?"

Aisha snuggled closer to him on the sofa. "I'm just trying to get to know you."

"You know all you need to know."

"You're like Abe. You only let me know what you want me to know. Everything else is a secret. He used to shut down on me and wouldn't talk."

Lorenzo stared at the blonde-haired beauty. He liked Aisha. He even thought he was falling for her, but she could be very annoying. She talked too much, and she could be whiny. But nevertheless, she was a bitch that Abe used to fuck with. "You wanna know a secret?" he asked her.

Aisha smiled big while nodding her head.

"Okay but you gotta give me some head first," he said with a teasing smile. Just as he figured Aisha didn't waste any time getting to business. Now Aisha's dick sucking skills were on point. He knew Abe had to be missing that. Sweet little Lovely didn't look like the type that sucked dick. Thinking of Lovely made him moan. His dick hardened even more. He still remembered how tight her little virginal pussy was when he took it. She tried to fight back but she was bound, and he had her pinned down. He would love another chance to get back up in that. Lovely was still just as pretty as she was at fifteen. Lorenzo could see himself fucking the shit out of her and shooting his cum on her. That would fuck Abe up.

Lorenzo had never cared for Abe's existence even as small children. His uncle Esau used to call Abe the devil. That was why Abe's real name was Abaddon which was one of the devil's aliases in the Book of Revelations. Abe always thought he was better because of his light skin, blue eyes, and pretty boy looks. As teenagers, Abe got all of the girls, all of the praise from Antino, and more opportunities than Lorenzo did. It was like Lorenzo had to work harder to prove himself to Antino.

Lorenzo ended up in prison on drug charges years later while Abe remained free getting his education and pretending to be a good guy. But now, the shit was playing catch up. It was time for Abe to fall. That was exciting enough to make Lorenzo bust his nut.

The thing Lorenzo loved about when Aisha gave head was that the bitch loved swallowing. She made sure she got every last bit of it. After Aisha was finished, she popped her head up and said, "Okay. Tell me the secret."

Lorenzo chuckled. "Okay. Check this out. What I'm about to tell you stay between us. You understand?"

Aisha nodded.

"A'ight. Me, Abe, and Eric robbed and killed ol' girl's mama and daddy. That bitch was supposed to die too, but she didn't. She just lost her vision or some shit."

"Who? Lovely?" Aisha asked in disbelief.

"Yeah. Abe know who the fuck she is too, but that mu'fucka still married her. Ain't that some foul shit?"

Aisha was stunned. "I can't believe that. You're gotta be wrong."

"I'm dead serious. That's why Abe gave me that money. And he finna give me some more if he wanna keep his secret away from Lovely."

"And what if he doesn't wanna give you money anymore?"

Lorenzo said, "I wanna kidnap that bitch." He reached over to the nightstand and retrieved the half-smoked blunt and lighter. He lit it up and began inhaling the contents of the blunt.

"You're not gonna hurt her, are you?" Aisha asked.

"As long as she don't act out of order," he said. He looked at Aisha. She was evil, conniving, vindictive, and shady but she was concerned about another bitch's safety. "Why you care anyway? You getting soft on me like that nigga Abe ain't you?"

"No. I just...I don't know," Aisha stated taking the blunt from him. She asked, "Why you call Abe soft?"

"Cause twelve, fifteen years ago he wouldn't have let a nigga like me live. A nigga threaten him in any kind of way was as good as dead."

"Abe was knocking niggas off like that for real?" Aisha asked.

"Hell yeah."

"So how we gonna do this and how much we asking for?"

"I want five million. We can split it."

"You honestly think Abe will come off that much for Lovely?"

"I know he will. I can see the desperation in his eyes whenever I speak on it."

Aisha looked at Lorenzo in awe. She couldn't believe he felt confident enough to go against a force like Abe.

"I gotta speak to someone else on this matter first," Lorenzo said.

"Who?"

"Stop asking so many questions. Damn!"

Aisha began to think how she could capitalize on this situation herself. Abe had plenty of money to give away. Aisha thought, maybe I can get my old love back.

———

Kiera tried to stifle her cries as she was being pounded from the back. Her cries of pleasure coincided with the bumping of the bed. She wanted to tell him he was being too rough, but it was how she liked it.

"You like that?" he asked in between pants. "You like this dick?"

"Yesss," Kiera answered. He kept her lowered by placing his hand on her back. She was pinned and couldn't move much. She grabbed handfuls of her sheets and muffled her cries in her pillow.

His stroked became stagnant as he buckled behind her. He was cumming. Kiera almost didn't want it to end. After he pulled out of her and collapsed on the bed, she remained in the position. She looked at him. He was sweating, and his fine hair was wet and sticking around his hairline. "That shit was good."

He smacked her ass that was still tooted in the air. "This pussy was good."

"Make me a sandwich and get me some juice," Kiera told him playfully.

"Yeah right," he said.

"How do you feel?"

He motioned his hand in a "so-so" manner. It was Monday mid-morning. Two days after Eli learned that the man that he's always known to be his father might not be his father. When it came to his mother, there was nothing to put past her though. Eli was madder than hurt. He was mad because of the way they were treated, especially Abe. Perhaps if their real father had been in their lives, they would know how it felt to be loved by a father.

The doorbell rang. Then there was pounding on the door. The doorbell sounded off again. Ugh, Eli thought. That was the thing about living in a bigger house. He would have to get out of the comforts of his bed and travel all the way to the downstairs foyer. What possessed Abe to design this house like this, Eli thought?

His phone started ringing. He looked at it. It was Robin. Shit! He looked over at Kiera who was not sleep but had her eyes closed. He said, "I'll be right back." He hurriedly dressed in his clothes.

"Sounds like you have a crazy person at your door," Kiera mumbled.

Eli went the distance to answer the door for Robin. "Hey. What are you doing here?"

"Is Kiera here?" Robin asked. She knew Kiera was because her car was parked under the portico behind Eli's vehicle.

Eli looked outside ignoring Robin's apparent bothered mood. "Is it trying to rain?"

Robin brushed past him quickly before Eli could stop her and went up the spiral stairs to the main floor. She waited for Eli to join her. She folded her arms over her chest, "Where is she?"

"She's in here somewhere," Eli said.

"She shouldn't be here," Robin said firmly.

"Well, we are trying to work out a friendship in relation to the twins."

Robin gave him a doubting look. Eli could tell she was upset.

"You smell like sex," Robin said finally.

Eli didn't know how to respond to that. He began to walk away, "I'll be right back."

Eli entered his bedroom to discover Kiera was already dressed and sitting up. "So, what does Robin want?"

"How you know it was her? She's been texting my phone like crazy. Anyway, I'll be back." Eli went into his bathroom.

"That bitch is foul," Kiera said under her breath but hoped that Eli heard it.

"What are you talking about?" Eli asked appearing back in the bedroom.

"Your friend. I hope you ain't tryna be with her for real? Eli, you have no idea. That bitch is shady. You don't need to be with her."

Eli looked at her blankly. "I'm not being with anybody. But why do you keep saying that about her? Do you know something about Robin or something?"

"That bitch ain't no good," Kiera mumbled getting up from the bed.

Eli asked, "Where are you going?"

"Out there," she said. She looked at Eli with a smirk. "I ain't gon fuck with your girlfriend."

Eli gave her a look that read he didn't trust her. "Don't start no shit, Kiera. I'll be out there in a minute."

Kiera walked down the hall seeing Robin standing there with her arms folded across her chest. A sinister grin spread across Kiera's face as she neared her.

Robin turned to face Kiera and asked, "Why are you even here?"

"To warn him about you. Eli needs to know you ain't no good."

"Like you are?" Robin countered.

"But you're fucking his daddy."

Robin's eyes widen, and she gasped in shock.

Feeling like she was one up on Robin, Kiera nodded knowingly. "Uh huh. I know about your shit."

Robin remained quiet questioning Kiera with her eyes only.

Kiera taunted, "Whatcha gotta say now?"

Thinking quickly Robin said, "But you're plotting against Abe and Lovely."

"I'm not doing shit," Kiera said with disdain.

"And who you think they will believe?" Robin asked snidely.

Kiera didn't have a comeback.

"My point exactly. So, keep your mouth shut, and we both can get what we want out of this," Robin said.

"Which is what for you?"

"I want all of the money I can get out of this. My mama sick and don't have good insurance."

"And I'm supposed to be sympathetic?"

"You ain't gotta be anything," Robin said looking down her nose at Kiera. "Anyway. Are you over here fucking Eli?"

"Why?"

Robin laughed wryly, "I ain't worried about it. Eli doesn't wanna fuck you anyway."

"But he already did."

"Yeah, ten years ago," Robin said flippantly. Eli started down the hall approaching them.

"Naw bitch. Recently," Kiera said smartly.

"Recently?"

"That's what I said. He was all up in this pussy just fifteen minutes ago."

Out of nowhere, Robin lunged for Kiera and connected with her cheek. Kiera went for Robin's hair and yanked her as hard as she could. Robin's head went down, but it didn't stop her from swinging her arms wildly in hopes to land a few slaps.

Before it could totally register with Eli, the two girls were in a tangled fist fight. "Y'all stop this shit!" He managed to get in between them and pry them out of each other's grasp.

Robin pulled away, panting, "I hate that bitch!"

Kiera straightened her hair and clothes. "Feelings mutual hoe."

"You the hoe. You fuck every damn thing if you think it'll benefit you, you fucking whore!"

"Fuck you!" Kiera grabbed the vase sitting on the table next to her and flung it at Robin.

Eli's eyes widened in disbelief. "Kiera!"

"The bitch act like she was finna hit me," Kiera explained.

Eli snapped, "You know good, and damn well she wasn't about to hit you. You broke my fucking vase!"

Breathing heavily and nose flaring, Robin asked, "So is this what the problem is Eli? You fucking this bitch now?"

Kiera and Robin waited for the answer. Eli simply said, "I can't answer that right now."

"Okay then," Robin said. She walked over to the matching tall vase and pushed it over. "I'll just do what she did since it's alright."

"You lil bitch," Eli said in disbelief. Now he had two expensive Lalique Palazzo vases shattered on the floor.

"Fuck you, Eli!" Robin exclaimed in anger.

"I can't believe you just did that shit. Both y'all bitches done lost your goddamn minds!" Eli shouted. He was angered by both of their behavior. So much was going on he didn't even realize Abe was coming up the stairs.

"What's going on in here?" Abe asked.

"Damn, where you come from?" Eli asked.

Abe looked at the mess on the floor. "They're breaking shit, or did you do that?"

"They did this bullshit," Eli mumbled heading toward his kitchen.

Desperately Kiera said to Abe, "Can I talk to you?"

"Abe don't wanna talk to you," Robin answered. She shot daggers at Kiera daring her to open her mouth.

Abe said, "Not right now. I'll call you though." He walked off toward the den.

Robin glared at Kiera and spoke in a low voice, "I ain't leaving until you leave. And if you think about trying to tell Abe anything I will tell Lo to have your ass and them twins of yours killed."

"Bitch, you ain't gon do shit," Kiera sneered.

"Run your mouth then," Robin threatened.

Kiera didn't reply because Eli was coming back with a broom, dustpan, and trash bag. He handed Kiera the broom and dustpan. "Get this shit up. Every last piece."

Chapter Fifteen

I n his whole thirty-five years, this was the first Abe had ever despised his mother. He wasn't sure if he could forgive her, but he knew what David was telling him was right.

"Boys...you have to forgive that woman and move on," David said as he looked from one brother to the other. They were in his restaurant waiting for Sarah's arrival.

Abe said, ""But do you realize I was everything I was because of her lies?"

"I understand that," David said with a nod. "But from her perspective, I understand why she was unable to tell. Remember she was raped by Antino. That can mess a woman up. Look at Lovely for example. Speaking of Lovely how do you think she will feel once she finds out the truth? We've already discuss this. Wouldn't you want her to forgive?"

"That's bullshit," Eli mumbled under his breath.

Abe's eyes shifted to Eli. He totally agreed with Eli. He wasn't believing anything Sarah was saying. Abe answered David's question. "Lovely won't forgive me. She's gonna want me to burn in hell."

"She might, but you would hope she wouldn't. That's kinda what Sarah is hoping. If she's willing, I say make amends."

"I'm so angry with her though."

David chuckled. "Now Abe, you know you're not like that."

"That's the thing. With all this stuff coming out and people fucking with me I feel like I'm slipping into the old me. I don't want that David. I don't wanna ever go there again." Abe's eyes locked in on her mother walking in the restaurant. She saw him and started making her way over. "Here she is."

Sarah smiled when she saw David. "Hello."

David stood up to greet Sarah with a hug. "Hi, Sarah. You look nice today."

"Why thank you," She said sweetly as she slid in the booth next to Ike.

Eli rolled his eyes and focused on the traffic outside of the window.

Before parting, David said, "Let me know if you need anything."

There was silence at the table. Abe couldn't even look at Sarah. Eli refused to look at her. Ike stared her down.

"What?" Sarah asked with widen eyes.

"You tell us what," Ike responded. "We're waiting."

"Listen and let me explain okay?" Sarah said.

Without looking at her, Eli spoke, "Nothing but lies all our lives. And to think of how you and Esau treated Abe. All this time you knew who his father was."

"I didn't," Sarah said. "Ike, you're the more reasonable one, and I just want you to hear me out."

Ike was taken aback. He looked at her directly and asked, "How do you know that?"

Sarah glanced at Eli and said, "Well I know how this one thinks."

"You damn right," Eli said angrily.

She looked over at Abe. "And this one...I just don't know what he's thinking."

"He's thinking his mother is a lying piece of trash," Ike said matter of factly.

Sarah sighed and shifted in her seat. "First I'm sorry to all three of you—"

"Bullshit! You knew what you were doing!" Eli blurted. "Can you imagine how Abe feel right now? All those years of Esau treating him like garbage because you said you were raped."

"I was raped, Eli!" Sarah yelled in a whisper.

"Oh, so Lu go around raping women and producing babies?" Eli asked smartly.

"It wasn't Lu. It was his brother, Antino. I thought Abe was Antino's child. And that man raped me. So, I was suffering with my own thing. I know I messed up and I can't change what's been done but please don't hold this against me."

Ike said with irritation, "That man didn't rape you, Sarah. You know that."

"He did so too," she argued.

"Don't you need to be saying this to Abe?" Ike asked.

Sarah held Abe's piercing stare for a second before looking away.

Before he got too emotional, Abe said, "I think I need to go. I'm not ready for this."

"Wait, Abe. I thought we were going to work at mending things," Sarah said.

"What?" Abe was in shock. "Lady, I hate you so much right now. You can open your mothafuckin mouth to talk about every goddamn thing else, but you couldn't bother to pick up a goddamn phone and tell me you know who my fucking father is. Fuck you, Sarah!"

Abe's outburst drew attention their way. Embarrassed Sarah whispered, "Can you lower your voice. We shoulda met somewhere else."

An angry tear rolled down Abe's cheek. He quickly wiped it away.

Eli was angry too, but he sympathized with his brother more. "See what you did?" Eli asked. "Abe hates you now. All these years all he ever wanted was for you to show him some love and you never did because he was supposedly a rape baby. You let Esau control you and control the way you interacted with your sons."

"I know, and I'm sorry," Sarah said. Her voice began to tremble. "Will anybody be understanding of what I was going through?"

"No. You were our mother. You were supposed to protect us, but you let us be Esau's whoop ass practice. Is that why he did it? He knew me, and Abe wasn't his?" Ike asked.

"Ike, Esau loved you, and you know it. He always thought of you as his, but the truth is...I was already pregnant with you when he and I got together. He knew Abe wasn't his cause of how he looked," Sarah explained.

Ike's brow furrowed in confusion. "Wait, what did you say?"

"You're definitely not Esau's child," Sarah said.

Abe said, "So tell me something Sarah, for Eli and me not to be Esau's children you were sleeping around on Esau huh?"

Sarah didn't say anything.

Eli asked, "Did Luciano know all of this time too?"

"Talk to him when you see him," she said.

"So how does this really make you feel Mama?" Eli asked.

"It doesn't feel good," Sarah sniffled. "I'm sorry, and I didn't want it to go down like this."

"I'm sure you didn't," Ike mumbled. It was funny how things could change just like that. What you thought you knew you don't know and what you don't know you just don't fucking know. That's how Ike was feeling.

"Okay, you don't have to forgive me today but know that I know your secrets," Sarah said to Abe.

"What does that mean? Are you threatening me, Sarah?"

"What happened to calling me 'mama'? And no, I'm not threatening you. I wouldn't do you like that. I've caused you enough pain."

"So why you bring it up?"

"Because it puts you in a very vulnerable position. And you believe in God. You know that in order to be forgiven, you got to forgive."

"Don't be getting all religious on me now Sarah."

"Mama," she reminded him.

"You are Sarah to me."

"Listen, Abe, I fucked up. I fucked up big time. Eli is right when he said I was supposed to be your mother first and protect both of you from Esau. I failed big time. I know you blame your childhood and how we treated you for the reasons you did all of the horrible things you've done. One of those things was what was done to Lovely. But know son, you can't keep running from it and buying people's silence."

"What are you talking about now?"

"You don't think I know. I'm not stupid Abe. I know you better than you think I do. I know how you think."

Abe didn't say anything as he pondered the thought of what Sarah was saying. Out of curiosity, he asked, "How do you know about the Lovely situation?"

Sarah was hesitant as she was trying to think of something. Abe could see her searching for a lie. It irritated him. "Listen, woman, don't be fucking with me right now."

"I'm not. You know Lorenzo don't know how to keep his mouth closed. Esau told me about it," she said.

"So, you knew who Lovely was too?" Eli asked.

"Not at first," Sarah quickly said.

Abe could sense Sarah was lying or covering up something. Whatever she was doing Abe didn't have time for it. He got up from the booth. "C'mon y'all. Let's go."

Sarah got up to let Ike slide out of the seat. She watched her three sons walk away from her. Fearing the worst, thinking that her lifestyle was threatened Sarah went after them. She caught up with them as they reached Eli's SUV. "Abe!"

Abe looked back at Sarah. "What?"

226

Sarah smiled up at her son. "Can I just say that I'm proud of you? I've always been; just couldn't show it. I can't believe I produced such a beautiful man."

"Whatever," Abe said dismissively.

Sarah looked over at Eli and Ike, "I'm proud of all of you. And I'm sorry. I hope this doesn't ruin our chances of having a good mother-son relationship."

Ike, Eli, and Abe stared at her blankly.

"Well, I wanted to let you know that I'm filing for a divorce and kicking Esau out," she said.

"Good. How does he feel about that?" Eli asked.

"He doesn't because he doesn't know. I think he's been seeing another woman. I really don't care. I'm in my fifties and ain't got time for it. Whoever she is can have his Stedman looking ass."

"We'll talk to you later Sarah," Eli said getting in the driver's seat.

As Abe turned to get in the vehicle, Sarah gently grabbed his arm and said, "Thank you for everything Abe. Thank you for loving me when I didn't love you back."

Abe didn't say anything. He wanted to keep his emotions under control.

Sarah said. "Thank you, and I love you. I want us to repair a relationship that never was. What do you say?"

Abe shrugged. "I don't know."

———

Ike didn't understand stupidity very well, which was why things between he and Melissa were becoming strained. His phone vibrated in his pocket. He pulled it out and looked at it. A smile crept across his face. He sat back in relax mode as he answered, "Hello?"

"Hey!" Jackie said cheerfully.

"Hey," Ike said. He looked forward to speaking to Jackie nowadays especially since Melissa had pulled away from him. Now he and Jackie spoke over the phone on a regular basis like the best of friends.

"What are you doing besides what you're supposed to be doing?" Jackie asked.

"Actually, I'm not even doing that," Ike said. He always loved talking to her. Jackie had a way of giving him good happy, carefree feelings. "So how has your day been going?"

"Good. I think Lovely's finna have me running all over the place," Jackie said.

"It's not that bad. I wish I had you and Eli's job. No, I take that back. Abe has Eli do everything. I'd be telling my brother, 'Nigga, go get it yourself.'"

Jackie giggled. "But your job is still easy. You work with your brother. Is Abe your boss?"

"Even though I'm the CFO, yes, Abe is my boss."

"At home, Abe is so different from this boss mode you complain about. I guess I gotta see it for myself."

"What about your boss?" Ike asked.

"You know Lovely is the best. I'm lucky to be working for her."

Ike's phone indicated he had another incoming call. He stared at the name displayed.

"Hello?" Jackie queried.

"Uh, yeah...I'm here. Can you hang on a second?" Ike put Jackie on hold to take the call from Melissa. "What's up and why are you calling me when you're just two doors down?"

"I didn't feel like getting up," she said. "Who are you talking to?"

"Why?" Ike asked snidely.

"Are you talking to Tomiko? Y'all making up? Or are you talking to that little girl."

"Why are you worried about it anyway? It doesn't seem as if you're ready to walk away from Reggie."

"It's not that simple, Ike."

"What's not simple about it, Melissa?"

A part of Melissa wanted to move on from Reggie, but her insecurities prevented her from having the confidence to move on with Ike. She knew Ike had a love for her, but she was afraid of not measuring up and being good enough for even him. Furthermore, she was scared of the unknown. She knew Reggie. She knew Ike, but not like a woman should know her man. Besides Reggie was starting to show a change. He wanted to work things out.

Ike knew those things were what Melissa wrestled with. He sighed. "So, I get left out there hanging?"

"I don't' want it to seem like that. But you had plans to leave Tomiko anyway, right? I didn't say I wanted you to leave Tomiko to be with me because I knew I wasn't sure of what I wanted. I know Reggie is an ass, and he hadn't always treated me right, but I'm willing to give him and me another chance."

"But he's cheating on you."

"He and I had a talk about all of that. He promises he won't step outside of our marriage anymore."

Was she stupid? "And you believe that?"

"I wanna believe it and give him a chance Ike," Melissa said.

Ike glanced at his cellphone. Jackie was still holding on. He said, "Okay Melissa. I'll respect that, and I won't bother you about us again." Ike added, "I want my son though."

Melissa looked at him desperately. "Ike, I can't."

"He's my son, and I want him to know I'm his father."

"Things are fine the way they are. I don't' wanna put Khy through all of that confusion."

"I don't want him to get eighteen and have resentment towards me because I wasn't there for him as a father either," Ike countered.

"He's crazy about you as his uncle. Now I will let him spend as much time with you as you want but as Uncle Ike."

"For now, I'll take that. But know that I won't sit back much longer. So, I suggest that you come up with a way to tell Reggie the truth. If you won't, I will."

————

Tomiko burst into the building disturbing the nice working atmosphere. Tomiko was furious about something. "Where's Ike?" she demanded. She was holding a large envelope.

"He's in his office. What's wrong?" Felicia asked with her face scrunched up.

Tomiko ignored her and stormed toward the direction of Ike's office.

Everyone stopped to be nosey and exchanged baffled glances. Even Abe came to his office door to see what the matter was.

Tomiko yelled, "You mothafucka! You gon' have me served on my gotdamn job. I ain't signing a mothafuckin thing! And how the FUCK you think you can have custody of my kids? You done lost your gotdamn mind!"

Tomiko threw the envelope at Ike and stormed out of his office. Ike grabbed the envelope and a small photo album and went after Tomiko. Before she could make it to the door, Ike called, "Tomiko!"

She turned around catching the album in her chest where Ike had slung it at her. The hit startled her and made some snicker. The album fell to the floor. Tomiko picked it up and started flipping through it. Ike approached her wearing a scowl of hatred and disgust. He offered her the pen he was holding. "Sign the goddamn papers."

Tomiko's whole tune changed. Her shoulders dropped with defeat and devastation. She softened, "Ike can we talk about this...I'm sorry...We can do counseling."

"Ain't that a bitch," Eli mumbled under his breath.

"What's in that album?" Felicia mumbled.

"I wanna see it," Eli snickered.

Ike wasn't moved by the crocodile tears Tomiko shed. "Sign these papers right now."

"Ike...Please!" Tomiko cried.

"Sign the fuckin papers," he said impatiently. He held the album up for emphasis. "I'm not going through another damn day of this with you. And I expect you out of my house by Sunday."

"Ike!" Tomiko cried.

Ike pulled the stack of papers out of the envelope. He placed them on the raised partition of the receptionist station. "The arrow tabs are where you need to sign."

Tomiko looked at him desperately. Ike held up the photo album. Tomiko reluctantly started signing in front of everyone watching.

Melissa was stunned. She stared at Ike as he made sure Tomiko didn't miss not one page. Melissa felt like she wasn't measuring up. He actually did what she should have been doing. Wow! She was really stunned.

When Tomiko walked out of the door with her pride and ego trailing behind everyone cheered and applauded.

"Thank you," Ike smiled with playful modesty. "Thank you so much."

"Can I see that?" Felicia asked grabbing for the album.

Ike held it away from her. "Nope. I'll let you look at it at a later date." Satisfied with his achievement Ike shot Melissa a look. She gave him a nod. He didn't know what that meant, but he hoped it meant she saw how serious he was about his situation. Hopefully, she would be inspired and do the same thing.

———

Eli looked up and saw bullshit walk through the door of the business office. *Great,* he thought. *Another trifling female.* He had already sit through his mother's bullshit for the day. Then Tomiko just showed her ass. And now here goes this tramp showing up to make the day complete. He stopped Aisha in her tracks before she could even open her mouth. "Abe is busy."

"I'm sure he is, but I need to talk to him," Aisha said haughtily.

"What part of busy did you not understand?" Eli asked with attitude.

From her receptionist station, Felicia quipped, "None of it I don't think."

Aisha rolled her eyes and sucked air through her teeth and exhaled heavily. "Seriously, this isn't necessary. Just tell him I need to speak with him."

"About what? Abe's a married man now," Eli said.

Felicia stood beside Eli. "What do you need me to do Eli?"

Eli said, "Call security. I don't know why she up here."

Aisha turned her nose up at Felicia with disgust. She looked at Eli, "Look, tell Abe he needs to see me, or I'll just talk to Lovely. Either way, it really doesn't matter to me. But I'm sure it would matter to Abe."

"What are you talking about?" Eli asked suddenly interested.

"Give Abe the message. He knows what I'm talking about," Aisha said with a smirk.

Felicia asked Eli, "Do you need security to escort this hoe away from here?"

233

Eli cut his eyes at Aisha and turned away from her. He said to Felicia, "No. Hold on."

Eli made his way to the boardroom where Abe was having a meeting with BevyCo board members. He tiptoed inside and walked over to Abe. He looked bothered by Eli disturbing him. Eli ignored it and whispered in his ear, "Aisha's out there. Said she need to see you. If you don't talk to her, she's going to Lovely."

Abe's whole demeanor changed. A look of worry crossed his face. He whispered, "She said that?"

Eli nodded. Abe sprouted from his chair excusing himself from the meeting. Eli followed him out. When Abe saw Aisha standing in the reception area wearing a smug grin, his eyebrows furrowed, and he glared at her. He motioned for Aisha to follow him. Eli wondered what that was about. He wasn't the only one. They all exchanged confused looks.

In Abe's office, Aisha sat opposite of Abe at his desk. She was still wearing her smug grin as she stared back at him. For some reason, he was finer than ever. He was letting his hair grow some; therefore, it formed into a wavy pattern. He seemed thicker, and his skin was brighter.

"What did you tell Eli?" he asked.

It was apparent he was upset and bothered. Aisha said, "That scowl on your face isn't becoming."

"Aisha don't play. I ain't got time for it," he said losing his patience in the process.

"Okay. I'll get to the point," she said. "I'm in need of some money, and you're gonna give it to me."

"And why is that?" he asked.

"Because I know something about you that you don't want Lovely to know," she said.

The smile on her face was annoying the hell out of Abe. He wanted to smack her but what would that solve? *Now how in the hell does she know about this*, Abe wondered. That was three people now plus his mother. Abe wondered if Sarah had told Esau.

Abe asked, "What do you know?"

"Do you really want me to say it out loud?"

"What do you know?" he repeated, this time with more firmness.

"That you, Lo, and Eric were the ones that killed Lovely's parents and did that to her. You also raped Lovely."

"I didn't rape Lovely."

"They said you would deny it too."

"Who the fuck is they?" Abe asked growing irate.

"Don't worry about that part. Now I can go to Lovely with this information, or you can give me what I came for?"

"I'm not giving you shit. In fact, I'm getting tired of you mothafuckas coming at me with this bullshit. Get outta my office!"

"Are you sure you wanna do this?" Aisha asked.

No, he wasn't sure, but Abe was mad. How did he let himself get in this predicament? If they kept this up, he would go broke. Abe countered, "Are you sure you wanna do this?"

"I'm doing it."

"Okay. Let me explain something. With each time y'all come to me, it pisses me off. I'm really at the point where my old ways will come to handle this. And Aisha, that's something you do not want. I'm telling you; you don't want that. So, I suggest to you to please get up out of that chair and walk your ass out of my office and out of my building."

"Are you sure?" Aisha asked. She continued to sit firm and un-waivered. Inside she wanted to do exactly what he suggested. She didn't know what Abe was capable of doing. All she knew was she had never met that side of him.

Abe thought of Lovely and the devastation she would endure once she learned the truth. He didn't want her agonizing over that. He would have no choice but to protect her from the truth. Abe asked, "What are you asking for Aisha?"

"First let me say, I miss you terribly. I was thinking that maybe we could spend some time together."

"Are you out of your goddamn mind?" Abe asked in disbelief. "I ain't being with you. I'd rather lick shit."

Aisha snickered, "Okay. So, you don't want me anymore. How about five million dollars and you'll never hear from me again."

"Five million?"

"That's reasonable considering Lovely's life is priceless," Aisha said.

"What do you need five million dollars for?"

"I wanna secure my future."

Abe blew out air in frustration. He hated being at someone else's mercy. It was usually the other way around. "I can't," he said. "Maybe five hundred thousand."

Aisha shook her head. "Uh-uh. Five million. This is a once in a lifetime opportunity for me."

"What if I just kill you instead?" Abe asked pulling out his .45 magnum and sitting on the desk for emphasis.

Aisha started shaking fearfully. "Abe, stop playing."

He loaded a round in the magazine and pointed it towards her. Coldly he said, "Get outta my office."

This time Aisha didn't hesitate to get up from the chair. She said, "I'll call y—"

Aisha's words were cut off by the loud bang of the gun going off. She thought she was hit, but she realized she was still up and able to walk. Aisha ran out of Abe's office almost knocking down those who were running to Abe's office to see what had happened.

Abe shot the ceiling, but he wanted to kill Aisha so bad. Seconds later his office was filled with his staff and the board members that were at the meeting.

"What is going on?" Luciano asked. He eyed the gun still in Abe's hand.

"Did you just try to kill Aisha?" Eli asked before cracking up with laughter.

"That ain't funny!" Ike said angrily.

"Yeah, it is," Eli laughed. "I hate that hoe."

Antino approached a very disconcerted, very distressed, and frustrated Abe. Abe had an unhinged look in his eyes that Antino knew all too well. "Give me that gun Abe."

"I wasn't going to shoot her," Abe finally said. "I needed the bitch out of my office."

"What was this about?" Luciano wanted to know.

Antino took Abe's gun and handed it off to security. He said, "Can everybody get out for a second?"

Eli was still laughing. His laughter was contagious causing the others to laugh too.

Ike asked before walking out, "Will you be okay?"

Antino nodded and waved them off. He shut the door behind the last person. He turned to Abe who had gotten up and went to his window and stared out. This was something Abe always did when he was heavily bothered. Antino asked, "What is it, son?"

Abe turned to Antino, "They're fuckin with me. Now, this bitch knows and asking for five million mothafuckin dollars."

"Who? The lady that was running out of here?"

"Yes. Aisha, my ex. I don't even know how the fuck she knows. What the fuck am I gonna do?"

"Well, we can take care of it, Abe. Just give me the word," Antino said.

"I'm trying my hardest not to go back to that Ant. I swear I don't wanna do that kind of stuff," Abe cried.

"Well, it's either that or tell Lovely. That will mean the Prasads will know too. They will have us killed."

Abe got up abruptly. "I gotta get outta here for a few days. This shit is fucking with me again."

"Take a few days off. We'll hold the fort down."

———

Aisha, still shaken waited until she was down the street before calling Lorenzo.

"Hello," he answered.

"That bastard just shot at me!" she exclaimed angrily.

"Who?"

"Abe!"

"What did you say, Aisha?"

"I went in there like you instructed me to. I made the threats. He wasn't going for it at first then he thought about it. I told him the amount, and that's when he pulled out the gun."

"And he shot at you?"

"He told me to get out then shot at me."

"So, he missed on purpose if you're able to call me," he chuckled.

"This shit ain't funny Lorenzo. From now on, you do all of the face to face."

"Chill mama," he laughed. "I can't believe that nigga shot at you though. But listen, I bet he'll wanna do it. He just tryna put a little fear in you."

"So, what do we do now?"

"We wait a couple of days to see if he reach out to you."

"And if he doesn't?"

"Plan B."

Chapter Sixteen

Eli hadn't spent time with Kris in a while. Just being in her company now was refreshing for Eli. With her sitting so close, made him realize just how much he missed her. Sometimes Eli craved those quiet, intimate moments he and Kris used to share.

Kris was laughing, "That bitch was scared."

"I wish you could have seen her running up out of that office. Abe was just sitting there like he hadn't done a thing," Eli giggled.

"I wish I had been there," Kris said.

Eli looked into Kris's eyes and just appreciated the sight of her. "I miss you."

Kris blushed with a smile. She said quietly, "I miss you too."

"Are you seeing anybody?"

Kris shook her head.

"Do you miss being with me?"

Kris answered, "You know I do."

Eli had only one thing on his mind. That was being sexually pleased. He asked in a soft, seductive voice, "You gonna spend the night with me?"

Kris gave Eli an incredulous look. "You can't be serious."

"I am."

"What about that thang you've been messing with?"

"We're just friends. Ain't nothing going on with that."

"Eli you're lying," Kris chuckled. "I know you. Your eyebrow goes up when you're lying."

Eli started laughing. "No, it doesn't."

"It does. It's going up right now."

In their laughter, Kris's hand landed on Eli's thigh. Eli stopped laughing and gave Kris a knowing look. Eli asked in a whisper, "You wanna taste it?"

Kris shook her head with a slight smile. "No. I didn't come here for that."

"Yeah you did," Eli teased.

"No, I didn't," Kris sighed. She looked at her watch for the time.

"You gotta go already?"

She nodded. There was a sadness in her eyes.

Eli's expression mimicked hers. He said softly, "You don't have to go. You can just stay here."

"I can't. I gotta get back to North Carolina," she said. She held her head down as she went into deep thought of what to say next.

Eli wanted to pull her close and hold her tight begging her not to leave him again, but the idea of doing that felt out of his character. It actually made him feel funny in his gut. It was nervousness and anxiety. Here he was in the company of a woman who he knew he had feelings for, but he was unable to express that, therefore, risking losing her again. There was no telling when he would see her again. This was the time to let her know how he felt.

Kris stood up and stretched. "I need to get going. Can you walk me out?"

"You know where the door is," Eli replied dryly.

Kris gave Eli a look. "Eli, really?"

Eli reluctantly got up. "C'mon."

Kris followed him down to the foyer. When they got to the door, Kris turned to Eli. Nervously she said, "Before I go, there's something I need to tell you."

"What?"

Eli could sense that it was difficult for Kris to come out with what she needed to say. His first thought was she had a disease that she possibly passed on to him. "Kris, you bet not have given me anything."

"No Eli. It's nothing like that...well...maybe," Kris said with a teasing smile.

"What the fuck that mean?" Eli asked seriously. Through the glass panels, he could see a car pulling up under the portico caught his attention. He wondered who it could be since only a few people had his access codes to let themselves in.

Kris turned her attention to the door just as the person on the other side began to pound the door while ringing the doorbell.

Eli opened the door. Irritated he snapped, "What the hell is wrong with you?"

Sarah looked surprised and was still in mid-knock. She looked at Kris, then back at Eli. She cleared her throat and straightened her posture. "Didn't realize you had company."

Eli rolled his eyes in exasperation. "Mama, what do you want?"

"I'm sorry to interrupt," Sarah said glancing over at Kris again, "but I need you to take me somewhere."

"Huh?" Eli said growing more aggravated by the minute. Ever since the whole blow up at the Labor Day party, Eli has had very little patience when dealing with his mother.

"I need you to take me somewhere," Sarah repeated. "And we gotta move fast. Like right now. C'mon!" She turned away to head to his SUV.

Eli stood there staring at Sarah like she had lost her mind.

Stepping outside Kris said, "I guess I'll call you or something."

"No, tell me what you have to tell me."

Looking over at an anxious Sarah, Kris chuckled, "It's not that serious. Take care of your mother. She looks like she's about to explode."

Eli looked over at his mother who was motioning him to hurry up. He cut his eyes at her in detest. He looked back at Kris, "You make sure you call me."

Kris nodded. She opened her arms for a hug. Eli was hesitant, but he submitted. She was so tiny in his arms. He wanted to hold her forever. He forced himself to release her and pull back.

Kris smiled, "I still love you, Eli."

"I...uh...I still love...," he stammered.

Kris chuckled. "Don't worry about it. I know you love yourself as always."

———

"Dammit!" Robin thought. It was time for her to make a payment from Lovely's account to her made-up charity recipient. She wasn't able to access the account online as she had before. Something had to be wrong.

Robin left her bedroom in search of Lovely. She found her in the conservatory standing by the windows, singing low and soft to AJ.

"Lovely!" Robin called.

Startled, Lovely turned towards Robin. "You scared me."

"Sorry," Robin mumbled. She stared at AJ trying to position his fist just right at his tiny mouth for suckling. His bright eyes had changed to be the exact blue as his father's. He was indeed a beautiful baby. Robin wished she could be AJ's mother.

"What do you need?" Lovely asked.

"Oh," Robin said snapping out of her thoughts. "I just wanted to tell you that I was unable to get into the account online."

"That petty account?" Lovely asked for clarity.

"The one I was overseeing for you."

"Oh, I closed that account," Lovely said. "My new financial advisors advised me to do so. They were looking over some things and wanted to make sure my money was where it should be and doing what it should be doing."

Robin asked, "Well what about some of the organizations you had me draft checks to from that account?"

"The advisors are looking at those and will be handling that for me too," Lovely answered.

Robin didn't know if she should worry or be angry. She was feeling more of the latter being that her plans were cut short. "It would have been nice if you had told me."

Confused and taken aback, Lovely said, "I didn't think it was a big deal."

"I mean, there could have been a pending transaction," Robin went on. She could imagine Esau ranting about this news.

"There wasn't I'm sure," Lovely said. She began to walk towards the door. "Was that all you needed?"

Robin mocked Lovely behind her back. She said, "Yeah, I guess so."

"Well, I'm about to put this lil man down so he can be well rested and ready for when his daddy comes home," Lovely cooed.

Robin rolled her eyes upward. She followed Lovely out of the conservatory. "Lovely, there is one more thing."

"What is it?"

"Do you know if Eli and Kiera got something going on?" Robin asked.

This made Lovely laugh a little. "I'm not sure. I know they've become friends which was a feat in itself."

"Well, how do you feel about Kiera now? I noticed that the two of you carry on like the way we used to."

"She's a cool girl," Lovely said. Robin continued to follow her to the baby's nursery.

"Is she replacing me?" Robin asked.

Lovely placed AJ in his bed. After assuring he would be content on his own, Lovely stood fully to address Robin. "What do you mean by that?"

"I just feel like you don't need me for anything anymore. And you've become close with Kiera. And then there's Jackie being here. I just feel like I'm not needed for anything anymore."

"Well, I don't need you as much anymore. Not here in the house at least," Lovely said. "It's a good thing, right?"

Robin shrugged, "I guess. It's just I'm used to being your right-hand woman."

"And you will be when things start taking off with me and Abe's foundation." Lovely smiled to Robin before walking away.

Robin looked down at AJ who was already drifting off to sleep. He was such a perfect baby just like his perfect parents. It made Robin nauseous.

Following behind Lovely, Robin said with thought, "Abe. You're really in love with him, huh?"

Lovely looked back at her with a grin. "Of course, I am."

"How much do you really know him?" Robin asked.

Instead of answering Lovely asked defensively, "Why are you asking me that?"

Robin was nonchalant in her reply. "Oh, nothing. Sometimes we just don't know who people really are. You know, most people have skeletons they'd rather keep in the closet."

Unfazed by Robin's insinuation, Lovely shrugged. "I really don't care at this point."

So foolish, Robin thought. "Well if you don't need me for anything I'll be on my way. I'll call you if I plan to spend the night away."

Lovely nodded. The way she did it translated to Robin as if she could care less. Robin was beginning to resent Lovely more and more as each day passed.

————

Eli was annoyed with his mother. He had tuned her out for most of the ride. All he knew was she had mentioned something about catching Esau in the act. Eli didn't care to hear any of it. Sarah's and Esau's problems were exactly that: their problems. So, what if Esau was cheating. Didn't Sarah mention she was divorcing Esau anyway?

"Eli, are you listening to me?" Sarah asked.

"Uh huh," Eli murmured absently. His mind drifted to Kris wondering what she had to tell him.

"Right here!" Sarah exclaimed. "Turn in the lot."

Eli pulled into the parking lot of the high-rise condominiums. He backed in a parking spot so that they could have a good view of the front entrance. "Don't you need an access code to get in the building?"

"I have it," Sarah boasted.

"So, what are we doing exactly?" Eli asked.

"Your daddy don't think I know, but he bought a condo in this building. This is where he be bringing his little whores."

"But why do you care? Aren't you filing for a divorce?"

"Because he was talking shit the other day about he married me under false pretenses or something. He keeps bringing up the whole Lu and Antino thing. He acts as if he's so innocent."

"So."

"But Eli. I need for you to see who his little whore is," Sarah said with a sly smile.

"Who is it?" Eli asked.

"You'll see," Sarah said looking toward the building's entrance.

Eli looked around the lot and noticed a very familiar late model white Impala in the visitor's parking space. It couldn't be, he thought.

Sarah excitedly slapped Eli on the shoulder repeatedly. "Look!"

Coming out of the building was a man and a woman. The woman was angrily marching to her vehicle which happened to be the white Impala. The man was right behind her. He seemed to be arguing with her about something, and she wasn't trying to hear it. She was upset.

Eli spoke his thought out loud, "What the fuck is she doing with Esau?"

Chapter Seventeen

Abe looked down at his son. Such a tiny little thing that depended on Abe and his mother to care for him. Abe was still proud of his offspring. He smiled as he watched AJ struggle to get his fingers in his mouth. "Are you hungry? Lovely when was the last time he ate?"

"I ain't thinking about AJ," Lovely said playfully. "That little boy can eat. He ate about an hour ago."

"He's gonna be big like me," Abe said proudly.

"You think so?" Lovely asked. AJ started making whiny noises.

"I know so. I can see it in his hands and feet. And let's not forget his lil wang."

Lovely started laughing as she nudged Abe. "Stop it! You're so silly."

Abe laughed too. "I'm serious. My son is blessed."

The smile on Lovely's face faded as she was about to say something she was dreading.

Abe was concerned. He frowned, "What's the matter, baby?"

"There's something I need to tell you."

Ivy Symone

"What is it?" AJ began to fuss. Abe went into immediate soothing mode as he rocked and pat his son on his back. AJ calmed down.

"I think I'm pregnant again."

"What?"

"You heard me," she said coyly. "We didn't wait until the six weeks were up Abe. I told you to wait."

"Lovely..." he let his voice trail as he took the news in.

"You're upset," Lovely said quietly. "I know it's too soon and—"

"I hope you have twins this time," Abe said with a chuckle.

Lovely lifted her face in his direction. "What?"

"I want as many kids as you're willing to have. I didn't think you would get pregnant so soon. But hell, we can afford to have as many as we want."

"You're not upset?"

"Why would I be?"

"I mean we're just now getting used to his little butt."

"Okay. We have Aunt Livy, Lulu, Robin, Jackie, and Grace. Melissa will come and help out too. But if I need to, I'll hire as much help as we need."

Lovely joked, "I think AJ wants to be the only baby around here though."

Abe said, "I think he was just sleepy." He pulled AJ from his shoulder to look at him. AJ was knocked out.

"There's something else I wanted to talk to you about," Lovely said meekly.

"What is it?"

"I asked my uncle to look into who was responsible for my parents' death, my rape and the loss of my vision."

Abe tensed up. "Yeah?"

"I wasn't sure how you would feel about it. But I just want closure that I never got."

"So, what's your intentions after you find out who done it?"

"I don't know."

Abe got out of bed to transfer AJ from his arms to the bassinet in their bedroom's sitting area. He came back pulling Lovely into his arms. "Baby, I think you need to leave that alone. I think it's risky, dangerous. And you don't know what these people are capable of doing."

"I know. And you're right. I just want their names."

"What's having their names gonna do?"

Lovely shrugged. "I just need something to close this for me. Besides one of them is Grace's real father."

"So, what do you want to do? Take him to court for child support? You want them to have a father-daughter relationship?" Abe asked with more attitude than he intended.

"Well, no...of course not."

Abe released her from his hold and laid down on the bed. "I'm a little insulted. I am Grace's real father. Fuck that nigga that did that shit to you. I'm here now. And I'll always be here."

"I know," Lovely said with uncertainty. "I'm sorry Abe. I wasn't trying to downplay your role in Grace's life. I was simply saying that I could at least have one of them arrested. They did do a rape kit on me. They have his DNA."

That was new information, Abe pondered. "They do?"

Lovely nodded. "All I need is one. That one will probably lead to the others."

"I'll talk to Mano about this. I don't want you stressing about this. Especially if you're pregnant."

Lovely smiled, "Okay."

Abe pulled her to him again. "Dr. Bradshaw is gonna wear us out."

Lovely giggled, "I know. But hey, it's good for business."

————

Ike looked at Melissa with disbelief. "You're doing what?"

"I'm putting in my two-weeks' notice with your brother, and I'm moving to Knoxville with Reggie."

"Not with Mekhi," Ike said.

"Yes, with my son."

"He's my son too, and I don't want him living that far away from me."

"It's Reggie's name on his birth certificate," Melissa countered matter of factly.

Ike narrowed his eyes at her, "But you and I both know that's not the truth."

"It doesn't matter Ike," she retorted smartly.

That pissed Ike off. "Like hell if it doesn't! That's my son. If anything, you should leave him here. I'll raise him."

"I'm his mother. Perhaps when he's a teenager, and he wants to be with my mother, then I'll let him come back."

"Don't do this," Ike begged. "Don't you wanna see what can become of us? I fucked up years ago by not choosing you. Don't do the same thing, Melissa."

"Ike, why do you care?" Melissa asked angrily. "You've got Jackie in your face all the time nowadays anyway."

"We're just friends. It's you I love," Ike said desperately.

Melissa asked, "Have you been fucking her?"

"Melissa stop being like this."

"Oh, so she is your little girlfriend. I knew it. I knew you were fucking around talking about how much you wanted me. I'm so glad I didn't fall for your shit."

"What shit? Baby, I want you. You're all I think about Melissa. I want you and my son to stay here. Let that mothafucka go back by his damn self,"

"No. He's my husband, and he wants to work things out with me," Melissa said.

"In order to work them out, he gotta move you out of town?" Ike asked.

There was a knock on the door. Thinking it was an employee with a quick question Ike called, "Come in."

Jackie pushed Ike's office door open. She looked at Ike then at Melissa. "Is everything good?"

"What are you doing here?" Ike asked with a smile. This was a total surprise.

"I decided to stop by to see you," Jackie said standing at his side.

Melissa looked on with disdain. "Really Ike? You can't get women, so you're getting with little girls."

"You know what? I owe you an ass whooping for pulling that bullshit you pulled last weekend," Jackie said.

"What's stopping you since you're big and bad?" Melissa challenged.

"No. Ladies not here, not now," Ike intervened.

Jackie said, "Out of respect for Ike I won't beat your big ass, but I want to say thank you though. If you hadn't done what you done, I wouldn't have ended up in bed with Ike."

Ike was shocked that Jackie would let something like that come out of her mouth.

Melissa came after both Ike and Jackie. Of course, Eli and Felicia came running into Ike's office to see what the commotion was. Melissa was hitting on Ike but was really trying to get to Jackie who was being shielded by Ike.

Eli shook his head. *What was up with these women fighting over him and his brothers?*

"Go on and leave now Melissa!" Ike shouted.

"Whatchu protecting the bitch for?" Melissa asked.

"I ain't letting you hit on her," Ike said. "Now go on. No, as a matter of fact, you don't have to return. Felicia, you've been promoted."

Felicia and Eli were shocked.

"You can't fire me. I'm Abe's assistant, not yours."

"I'm the acting CEO when Abe is out. You're fired for disruptive behavior to other employees and misconduct. I'm sending Abe and personnel an email now."

"Fuck you, Ike! You just mad cause I didn't want to leave my husband for you," Melissa spat.

Those listening were stunned.

"Sukie sukie now," Felicia said under her breath.

"That doesn't have anything to do with it. You can stay with that no good mothafucka. All I want is my son," Ike threw out.

Melissa grew angry. She was furious that he had called her out in front of everybody. "Mekhi is not your son so stop saying that shit!"

"What in the whole hell is this?" Felicia asked Eli.

"Stop asking questions and go pop some popcorn so we can watch this shit play out," Eli said with a chuckle."

Ike snapped, "Get outta my damn office. Everybody! Get the fuck out! Melissa get your shit and go. Felicia stay your black ass in here."

"I'm calling Abe," Melissa said swiftly exiting the office.

Ike turned to Jackie. "You sit your little hot ass down somewhere."

Jackie giggled as she made her way to Ike's small sofa. She looked up and caught him smiling at her. It made her smile even bigger.

"Why did you just tell that lie like that?" Ike wondered.

Jackie replied, "Technically it wasn't a lie. We did sleep in bed together that night. I didn't say that we had relations."

"But that's what she assumes."

Ivy Symone

Jackie shrugged nonchalantly, "So; let her think it. She needs to know she messed up and you don't have to wait around waiting on what she's gonna do."

"That I understand," Ike said walking over to her. He couldn't quite put his finger on it, but there was something he was definitely feeling about Jackie. Having romantic feelings for her would thwart his already complicated life more. However, there was a certain magnetism the younger woman had on him.

Uncomfortable with the way Ike was staring at her she got up and walked over to the big office window. As if a thought suddenly came to her, she suggested with excitement, "You know what you need? I think you need a vacation."

"I think I do too," Ike said.

"Then it's settled. Take one," Jackie said.

Walking closer to Jackie, he placed a hand on the small of her back in a gentle manner. It caused Jackie to let out a soft gasp.

Ike said, "I'll take one only if you accompany me."

Jackie's eyes grew big as she turned to him not quite believing what came out of his mouth. "Me?"

"Yeah you," Ike chuckled.

"When? I mean...Lovely...I just came and Lovely—"

"Don't worry about that; Lovely will understand," he said.

"Are you sure you want me to go with you?"

Ike nodded. He positioned himself close in front of her entrapping her between him and the window.

257

Jackie inhaled a nervous breath. She could feel her hardened nipples brushing up against him. His arms wrapped her close.

Ike said softly, "You're nervous. Relax."

"I'm trying," Jackie's voice quivered.

"Can I kiss you?"

Jackie's heart raced. So many thoughts and emotions were traveling through her mind and body. Men usually didn't handle her like this, but then again, she had never messed around with an older guy. Ike's tenderness came off as genuine though. He was sensual without being sexual. And Jackie even appreciated the fact he wasn't afraid to ask for what he wanted. His presence near her was almost a comfort that comes with security.

Jackie said in almost a whisper, "I guess."

Ike moved her hair away from her neck and placed a soft kiss right below her left ear.

He whispered, "Did you feel that?"

Jackie closed her eyes and exhaled. "Feel what?"

"Right. Something felt so right when my lips touched your skin."

———

That Saturday, everyone had gathered at Lovely and Abe's place just to unwind, relax and enjoy each other's company.

Abe noticed that Eli was drinking heavily, more than usual. "Slow down E."

"I'm straight," Eli said. He continued to sit quietly.

Abe became worried because this behavior was completely out of character for Eli. Something had to be weighing heavily on Eli's mind. Abe quietly asked, "You wanna go talk in private?"

Eli shook his head. "I'm straight."

"Are you sure?"

"Yep," Eli said. When he felt Abe still staring at him, he forced a laugh, "Abe! I'm fine. Go over there with your wife."

"Okay," Abe finally said before going to sit beside Lovely on the sofa.

Kam asked Lovely, "What's that you're drinking Lovely?"

"Oh, this is only cranberry juice," Lovely answered holding up her glass.

"What's up with that?" Kiera teased. "I noticed you were only drinking non-alcoholic drinks at the party."

Lovely blushed as she replied, "I'm not a heavy drinker anyway. Hell, I already can't see. My ass don't need to get too tipsy."

Abe looked at Kiera and questioned, "How you know what anybody was drinking at the party. Your ass was passed out."

Kiera laughed, "Man I know! I missed the fight and everything."

"I missed it too," Kam said.

"Lovely was in it," Eli joked.

Abe looked over at Eli. He was relieved to see Eli still being himself.

"Lovely was fighting?" Kam asked.

"I was not fighting," Lovely corrected.

"Man, that shit was funny," Eli laughed. "I won't forget that. And the look on your face Lovely. It was priceless."

"Hell yeah," Eric added. "If you hadn't been right there Eli, Lovely woulda kept going."

Lovely punched Abe on his thigh as a reminder of what she owed him for sending her spinning around the room that night.

"Baby, I said I was sorry. Eli shut up. Every time you bring that shit up Lovely starts beating on me," Abe said.

Kiera said playfully, "Beat him Lovely!"

Robin entered the room. She shot a couple of daggers Kiera's way before taking a seat beside Eli.

"Robin, you didn't get to see the fight either, did you?" Kam asked.

"No, but I heard about it," Robin said.

Kiera mumbled, "She had to leave to get to her lover."

Robin asked, "What did you say?"

Kiera smirked, "Nothing."

"You know Kiera, I'm really tired of your mouth," Robin said angrily.

"Don't talk to me hoe," Kiera sneered.

Eric whispered loudly, "Eli, getcho women!"

"Fuck them. Let 'em argue," Eli said dismissively.

"Damn, it's like that," Eric laughed.

"Neither one of them got much room to talk. Both of them are whores," Eli stated.

Abe looked at Eli. Was that the liquor talking?

"So, I'm a whore Eli?" Robin questioned.

"You're a needy whore," Eli said matter of factly.

Robin's mouth dropped open in shock. "Really Eli?"

Eli ignored Robin. He pointed to Kiera, "And that one. She's just a nasty whore. A whore who fuck people's daddies."

Kiera gave Eli a confused look. "What are you talking about?"

"Are you fucking Esau?" Eli asked bluntly.

Besides the music playing in the background, the room fell silent.

Kiera was taken aback. "No, I'm not fucking Esau." She glanced over at Robin. "Why would you ask me that Eli?"

"I saw you outside those condos arguing with Esau. It was you. Your car was there."

Kiera didn't know what to say. She had indeed been to Esau's condo, and they did argue in the parking lot. Desperately, she said, "It's not what you think."

"What I think is that you're a whore," Eli said getting up from where he sat. "I bet your nasty ass got worms for fucking with an old man."

Eric and Kam tried to stifle their laughter.

Eli looked at Abe, "I'm going home."

"You can't drive," Abe objected.

"It's just down the damn street," Eli pointed out.

"I'll drive him," Robin said.

"Wait!" Kiera exclaimed. She was on the verge of tears. "Don't I get to explain myself?"

Robin turned to Kiera with a smirk and said, "No one wants to hear it."

"She's the one that's—" Kiera was saying.

Eli interrupted her as a thought came to mind. "It's Esau isn't it?"

"Esau what?" Kiera asked.

"He's the twins' father," Eli stated knowingly.

"Eli, please let me explain!" Kiera begged.

"Kiera, is that true?" Abe asked.

Kiera felt ashamed. She was so disgusted with herself. Tears began to fall. "Can I explain?"

Eli shook his head pitying her. "I'm gone."

Robin hurried Eli out before Kiera decided to try to take some of the heat off herself and direct it at Robin.

Lovely whispered, "If I heard correctly, didn't Eli just call Robin a needy whore? Yet she's volunteering to take his ass home."

Kam grunted a laugh. "That's yo' friend Lovely."

———

A few days later Kiera sat in her car waiting for Eli to exit the business plaza. She and the twins had already been swabbed for DNA testing. Their part was finished. Instead of going home right away, Kiera waited for Eli.

When he walked out, she turned to the twins, "Don't get out of the car. I'll be right back."

Kiera hopped out of her car and hurried to catch up with Eli. "Hey!"

Eli rolled his eyes and kept walking towards his vehicle.

"Eli, wait. We need to talk."

"There's nothing to talk about." He stopped outside of his car.

She looked up into his eyes. "Listen, I'm sorry for all of this."

"Okay and what?" he said impatiently.

"Just hear me out," Kiera pleaded.

"I really don't wanna hear about how you fucked around with Esau."

"It wasn't like that. It was only a one-time thing. It happened around the time when you and I hooked up the first time. Remember when I was coming around all of the time trying to get with you?"

"You couldn't get me fast enough, so you fucked my supposed to be daddy?"

"No. He sorta forced himself on me."

"Oh Lawd! Another Sarah Masters. I ain't got time for this."

"No Eli! I'm telling the truth. I was so ashamed and felt so guilty I was afraid to tell anyone."

"And you shoulda felt ashamed, and you were guilty. You fucked the man who I've known to be my daddy for all of my life."

"I'm sorry. I mean, maybe I shoulda told you but I was afraid you would look down on me. And I would never have a chance with you."

"Well, you sure ain't got a chance now. And I was starting to like you."

"Eli, please. It's not like that."

"But you thought Esau was their daddy."

"Yes, I did. And to buy my silence, Esau has always sent me money to care for them."

"Okay, Kiera. I gotta go," Eli said opening his car door.

"Can we still be friends Eli?"

Eli shrugged. "I don't know. I'll think about it."

———

Kiera was grateful to Lovely for allowing the twins to spend the rest of the day with them. She needed a moment to herself to think things over. She was emotionally worn out as the past tormented her. She never wanted to hurt Eli, and she definitely didn't want to lose his friendship.

Before she was able to unwind, her doorbell sounded. She went to answer the door. She looked out of the peephole first. Frowning, she opened the door. "What are you doing here?"

"I was in the neighborhood," Lorenzo said as he stepped inside.

Kiera looked at him like he was crazy. "Excuse you. I don't remember inviting you inside. How the hell you know where I live anyway?"

"I have ways of finding out things," he said looking around the cozy apartment. "Nice place you have here."

"Thank you. Now, what do you want?" Kiera asked.

"Right now, I could use a drink. Whatcha got?" he asked as he began walking toward her kitchen.

Kiera rolled her eyes. She was not in the mood for company. Especially not the likes of Lorenzo. She followed him into the kitchen. "What kind of drink?"

"A soda will be fine."

Kiera went into her refrigerator to grab a soda. She handed it to him. When he took it, that's when she noticed he was wearing black leather gloves. It was warm outside. What was he doing wearing gloves?

"So, Kiera, have you told anybody anything about what you know?"

"What are you referring to?"

"My uncle said you might be a problem."

Kiera's mind immediately went to the day that Eli witnessed her outside arguing with Esau. "Why does he think that?"

"Cause you heard some shit you wasn't supposed to hear."

"But I already told Esau I wouldn't say anything."

"Robin doesn't seem to think you will keep your word."

"Oh, what the hell does she know." Kiera was growing agitated. She was ready for Lorenzo to go.

"She feel like you will tell just to get the heat off of you."

"I said I wouldn't tell. Is that why you came over here? To put some fear in me?"

"What did you hear exactly?" Lorenzo asked.

"I know Robin's been stealing money from Lovely."

"And what else?"

"Lovely closed the damn account," Kiera recalled. Kiera had gone to the condo to get some money from Esau. Before leaving, Kiera asked to use his bathroom. While in the bathroom, Robin showed up frantically rambling about the money situation with Lovely's account. Kiera heard all of it while in the bathroom.

"What else?"

An uneasiness settled over Kiera as she remembered the words she heard that day. "I don't even wanna say what else."

"Say it!" Lorenzo demanded.

"She said to Esau, 'Are you and Lo still gonna go through with kidnapping that bitch and killing her.' That's what I heard before Esau was able to shut her up."

Lorenzo looked around as if he was searching for signs of anyone else present in the house. "Where are your kids?" he asked.

"Not here," Kiera responded. She remained calm and cool, but a fear was bubbling inside her. She calculated in her head how quick she could grab a knife from the butcher block if he tried anything funny.

"What are you gonna do Kiera?"

Kiera looked at the can of soda that he hadn't bother to pick up once to take a sip. "Nothing."

"That's right. Nothing. And I'm here to make sure you do nothing."

Kiera stared him in his eyes and realized exactly what he was saying. She quickly turned to grab a knife, but he was on her before she could grab one. He grabbed the can of soda and bashed it in her face repeatedly to shut her up.

Dropping the can, he wrapped his hands around her neck and squeezed tightly. She clawed at his gloved hands as she struggled to stay conscious. Kiera looked him in his eyes and could see the thrill he got out of taking her life. The excitement danced wildly in his eyes. Her children came to mind, and she thought back if she had told them she loved them that day because she knew she would never see them again.

Chapter Eighteen

L ovely was so anxious. She couldn't be still longer than thirty seconds.

"Lovely baby, calm down," Aunt Livy said. She placed her hand on Lovely's bouncing knee.

"I can't help it. I don't feel good about this," Lovely said.

"Just pray about it. But there's no need in you working yourself up. Everything will be fine."

As much as Lovely wanted to believe Aunt Livy, her gut feeling told her that it wouldn't be fine. When Kiera didn't return to get the twins, Lovely knew something was wrong in that instance. It was now a whole day later and still no sign of Kiera.

"This is not good," Lulu said shaking her head. "Bad, bad feeling. She not answer phone. She no show."

Aunt Livy tried to dismiss Lulu with a wave of the head. Taking offense, Lulu said, "Don't wave hand at me. This is bad. Lovely knows."

"Okay, Lulu. But let's not make things worse," Aunt Livy said.

Robin walked into the den holding AJ. "You see who's up?"

"Give baby here," Lulu said reaching for him. "He no like you."

"He does like me," Robin said.

Lulu said, "If I no like, he no like."

Lovely snickered. "Really Lulu?"

Aunt Livy shook her head. "That little Chinese woman ain't got a lick of sense."

"I'm Laotian, not Chinese!" Lulu corrected.

"It's all the same to me," Aunt Livy mumbled under her breath.

Robin asked, "What's the word on Kiera?"

"As if you really care," Lovely said.

"Lovely, I take offense to that. Me and Kiera may have had our differences, but I wouldn't want nothing to happen to the girl," Robin stated.

"Lovely, that wasn't really a nice thing to say," Aunt Livy added.

Lovely wasn't going to apologize for it. Robin was probably hoping something had happened to Kiera.

"Abe is here," Lulu announced.

Grace, Bria, and Bryce all walked into the den. Bria asked, "Is my mama back yet?"

"No sweetie," Lovely said.

Grace went into the kitchen. "I just want some Funyuns."

Bria giggled. "Your breath is gonna stink!"

"Grace will have cootie breath," Bryce laughed.

Abe came through the door leading in from the garage. He looked at the kids in the kitchen. Aunt Livy could see the gloom in his face. She placed her hand on Lovely's shoulder and whispered, "Oh Jesus."

"Grace, can you and the twins go upstairs for a minute?" Abe asked.

"No problem," Grace said. "C'mon kiddos."

"Who you calling a kid?" Bryce asked as he followed right behind Grace and his sister.

Lovely got up and went to Abe. "What did you find out?"

Abe pulled Lovely to him and held her close. "She's dead."

"What?" the ladies asked in unison.

"What do you mean?" Lovely asked frantically.

Abe explained that Kiera was found in her home lifeless. Her death appeared to be due to asphyxiation as the results of a random, senseless home break-in. Lovely didn't take the news so well considering she had gone through a horrific tragedy very similar. Her heart hurt for Bria and Bryce. How could they tell them that they would never get to be with their mother again?

———

The following day should have been an exciting day, but due to Kiera's death, everyone was in a subdued state.

Lovely, Abe, Ike, Eli, Luciano, Cesar, and Sarah sat around the formal dining room table of Lovely's home. The results came back from everyone's DNA testing. Everyone was anxious to know what the envelopes would reveal.

Luciano looked at Abe and suggested, "How about you go first."

Abe looked down at the envelope from Genetic Assays. He was somewhat afraid of what was inside. Shaking the nervousness off, Abe proceeded with opening the envelope.

"What does it say?" Eli asked.

"It says that by a 99.99% probability that Luciano de Rosa cannot be excluded as my biological father," Abe answered. He looked over at Luciano. "Daddy?"

Luciano broke out in a huge grin. He got up, "Come here, son!"

Sarah was truly happy for Abe as she watched the two men hug each other. Abe deserved his father in his life. She felt horrible for keeping him from the truth for all of these years.

Cesar looked at Ike. "You're next."

Sarah was puzzled by the two envelopes Ike held in his hand. With her brow furrowed she asked, "Why are there two? You only tested with Luciano or did you test with Antino also?"

Ike shook his head. "No, I didn't test with Antino. I had Melissa's son tested."

"Melissa?" Sarah asked in disbelief. She thought she was aware of all of her sons' business, but this one had slipped by her. She asked, "Why would you need to test him? Is he your son, Ike?"

"We're about to find out," he mumbled as he opened the first envelope. A smile spread across his face. He looked over at Abe and stated, "You know, I knew there was a reason I always hated Esau."

Luciano grinned proudly, "So does that mean I'm your father?"

"Yes, it does," Ike said.

Luciano couldn't contain himself. Just as he had done with Abe, Luciano embraced Ike in the same affectionate, loving hug. Even Sarah had to dab at her eyes with some tissue.

Abe told Ike, "Get to the other one."

More anxious about what this envelope held, Ike opened it cautiously. He read it, but his expression wasn't as readable to everyone else. He simply folded the paper up and said quietly, "He's mine."

"That's great!" Lovely said excitedly.

Sadly, Ike said, "Yeah, but she took him. Give me a minute."

"It'll be okay Ike," Lovely tried to tell him in a comforting manner.

"Yeah, I know," Ike said as he headed out of the dining room.

"Melissa real fucked up for that," Eli voiced.

"Oh, shut up and get to yours," Abe said playfully.

Eli looked at the four envelopes in front of him. He didn't know which ones held what results. So, he just picked one. He opened it and read it. He looked up at their eager faces with great disappointment and said, "I'm not Lu's child."

"Figures," Sarah mumbled.

Eli opened the next one. He smiled as he read the results. "I told that girl! Bria is mine."

"Oh! Eli's a daddy!" Lovely squealed.

Eli opened the third envelope. He smiled again. "Bryce is mine too."

"Eli's a double daddy!" Lovely giggled.

Sarah smiled too. "Those are my grandbabies!"

"Okay get to the last one," Abe urged.

Eli exhaled heavily before opening the last one. He read the results. His brows furrowed with confusion and agitation. He looked at his mother. "Who the hell is my daddy?"

Sarah looked confused. She reached for the paper. "What did it say?"

"Antino ain't my daddy either!" Eli exclaimed angrily. "Who's my damn daddy if Lu and Antino isn't?"

Abe started laughing. "You ain't got no daddy!"

"Shut the fuck up," Eli snapped playfully.

Lovely chided, "Abe, that isn't nice."

"He ain't got no daddy. It's my turn to chant those words. He ain't got no daddy!" Abe taunted.

"I didn't say that shit to you!" Eli said.

"Yes, you did. When we were little," Abe said matter of factly.

"Boys stop it," Sarah said. She was irritated with the results. If Antino nor Luciano was Eli's daddy, then that left only one other person: Esau was Eli's actual father.

Sadly, Eli said, "Well I guess Esau is my daddy huh?"

Sarah nodded sympathetically.

Abe said, "I don't know what the problem is Eli. You've always thought Esau was your daddy anyway."

Eli sighed heavily. "It was just...I was just hoping I wasn't that man's child."

Luciano looked over at Sarah's troubled expression. "Are you okay?"

Sarah nodded. "I'm just glad it's over."

———

Four days later, Kiera's funeral took place. It was a sad day. Lovely hurt for the twins. Although they were gaining a father, it was painful to have lost their mother. Lovely knew that feeling all too well.

Grace tried to keep Bria and Bryce entertained as much as possible to keep their minds off the loss of their mother. For the most part, it worked, but they would have their moments when they realized Kiera wasn't coming back.

Kiera's mother, Sylvia wanted the twins to go back to Georgia with her. She made it known when everyone was gathered at Abe's and Lovely's for Kiera's repass. Sylvia was saying, "They'll be taken real good care of with me."

"I'm sure they would," Eli said with a smile laced with cynicism. "But I'm their father, and I'll be caring for them from here on out."

Bria was tickled. "Uncle Eli is our daddy?"

"Yeah dummy," Bryce said.

Eli cut in dramatically, and in a mechanical tone, he said, "No, no! Bryce don't call your sister dummy. Love one another. Now say you're sorry."

Everyone started laughing.

"How was that Lovely?" Eli asked with a proud smile. "Did that sound like a parent?"

"Oh, Lord! These poor babies," Aunt Livy said shaking her head.

Robin smiled, "Eli's gonna be a great father."

"Hey, I'm new at this. I'm learning," Eli said. "They potty trained right?"

"Eli, sit your ass down somewhere!" Lovely laughed.

"We been potty trained!" Bria said widening her eyes.

"But I bet you still piss in the bed," Eli said playfully.

"Bryce does," Bria giggled.

Bryce got angry. "No, I don't!"

Eli said, "It's alright Bryce. Your uncle Abe pissed in the bed until he was twelve."

"Fuck you!" Abe retorted.

"No curse words around my children," Eli chided. "Kids, tell Uncle Abe no-no!"

———

Abe, Ike, and Eric took a break from the post-reception and escaped to the study to discuss business. After about forty minutes, the door to the study opened and in walked Cesar. "Boys...," he said casually. He took a seat beside Eric. "Abe there's something I wanna discuss with you."

Eric got up, "I'ma go on downstairs and wait for you Abe."

"A'ight," Abe mumbled.

Cesar looked over at Ike. "Do you mind?"

Ike nodded, "Yeah cause anything you need to say to Abe you can say in front of me."

Cesar rolled her eyes with an exasperated sigh. Ever since the results of the paternity tests, it seemed as though Ike had become insecure as his role as Abe's older brother.

"This is sensitive matter," Cesar argued.

Abe told Ike, "Just give us a second."

Ike cut his eyes at Cesar as he got up from his chair. "Abe, I'd like a word with you before I leave in the morning."

"I gotcha," Abe smiled, humored by Ike's attitude.

Cesar waited until Ike left before speaking. "I need a big favor of you."

"What is it?"

Cesar removed a folded piece of paper from his breast pocket. He laid it on the desk. "You know the story behind what happened to Lovely. Her parents were shot execution style and set on fire. Lovely was shot in the back of her head which caused her blindness. She was also raped, and Grace is a product of that rape."

Abe's heart raced. He had to play it cool though. "Yeah, I'm familiar with all of that."

"Well, Lovely has always wanted to know who was behind that day. She used to want to seek vengeance, but it's just not in her to do so. She know all she gotta do is give the word and we'll have an army of men ready to take any and everybody down."

"Okay." Abe was growing nervous and started to squirm a little.

"Recently your wife reached out to her uncle and said she wanted to move forward with finding those responsible. She asked Mano to take care of it. Mano came to me."

Abe looked down at the paper. "So, what is this?"

"Well, I'm coming to you now. Remember when Papa said he had you researched when Lovely first got involved with you?"

Abe nodded.

"Well, I was in charge of that. The information came through me. I know what you used to do in the past."

Abe swallowed the lump that had formed out of nowhere in his throat. "What do you want me to do exactly?"

"I want you to take care of everybody on that list. That right there is a list of names of the people who took the man I considered an uncle and his wife from me."

Abe reached for the list cautiously. Surely his name couldn't be on this list. If it were Cesar wouldn't be talking so calmly. Abe unfolded the paper. He read the list from top to bottom: Fyah, Abaddon Masters; Ghost, Eric Barnes; and Loco, Lorenzo Harris.

"Do any of those names sound familiar?" Cesar asked.

Abe's eyes shot up to Cesar's menacing gaze. He explained, "I took the money and ordered everybody around. I didn't rape nor shoot Lovely."

Cesar sat back in his chair and stared Abe down.

Abe grew uncomfortable and nervous. His gun was in the desk drawer. If he needed to, he would put a bullet in Cesar's head.

Abe said, "I'll do whatever I have to, to make everything right. But please don't tell Lovely."

"I'm not. I love Lovely and would never want to hurt her in that way," Cesar said. "That would be too much for her to deal with."

"What are you gonna do to me?" Abe asked.

Cesar laughed heartily. "Nothing."

Abe was confused. He frowned, "I don't understand."

"Let me put your mind at ease," Cesar said as he leaned forward. "I was the one that hired you through Antino." Cesar sat back and let that information marinate on Abe's brain.

Abe was even more confused. He said, "So you've been knowing all of this time."

"Pretty much," he said. "Papa doesn't know. He doesn't need to know. Now I'm gonna continue to do this investigating and research. In the meantime, get your wife's mind off of this matter."

Abe let out the breath he didn't realize he had been holding.

Cesar smiled with easiness, "No worries. But it's a great thing he came to me first. Right?"

Abe nodded.

"So, who is Grace's father?" Cesar asked.

"Lorenzo."

"Okay. Well, I gotta get going," he said as he got up to exit the study. Before he left out, Cesar looked back, "Put that list up. And not a word to Papa."

"Okay."

Abe didn't know what to think of that. Here God was giving him a pass again.

———

Playing the perfect host, Lovely went around making sure that everyone was doing okay. Half of the people she didn't know; nor did she know who she was talking to most of the time. People were scattered everywhere in the house.

Lovely made her way into the formal living room. Someone touched her shoulder.

"Excuse me. Lovely, can I have a word with you?"

Thrown off and unsure of who exactly was before her, Lovely said, "Sure. Is everything okay?"

"Yeah, I'm fine. I'm gonna really miss my sister though."

Sister? Lovely began to think and then it came to her. The slender brown-skinned woman in front of her was Kenya. Lovely knew Kenya was Abe's ex, but she had never given Lovely any problems before like that damn Aisha. Lovely smiled, "Oh hey Kenya. I didn't realize you were here."

"Well, I just got here. I just wanted to stop by for a little bit and see my niece and nephew."

"That's nice because they need all of the love and support they can get right now. It's really sad to have to listen to them cry about their mother."

"Yeah, her murder was such a senseless violent act. People who go around murdering innocent people like that don't deserve their freedom. I hope they find the low life who took my sister's life."

"I hope so too."

"And I know that gotta really burn you up. Because weren't your parents killed by some random act of violence?"

There was something about Kenya's tone that Lovely couldn't quite put her finger on. It seemed rehearsed and rather disingenuous. "Yeah. Well, let me continue my rounds. Please help yourself to some food. There's plenty. The kids are upstairs now, but Eli is in the family room."

Kenya touched Lovely's arm again. "Wait. I wanted to ask you about your parents. Don't you want those people brought to justice too?"

Lovely said politely, "Well of course I do, but right now my focus is on Kiera's kids and making sure my family is safe."

"That's understandable. It's just that this whole violence thing is bothering me." She moved in closer to Lovely and said in a low tone where only Lovely could hear. "I think I know who done it."

Lovely whispered, "Who killed Kiera?"

"No," Kenya said. "Your parents."

This piqued Lovely's interest. "Who?"

In a sudden movement, Kenya stepped away from Lovely and cleared her throat. She said with a bright smile, "Thank you Lovely. I'm going to go see the kids now and fix me a bite to eat."

Lovely was confused as she watched Kenya's frame walk away from her.

"When did she get here?"

Lovely swung around and realized Abe had come up behind her. Lovely shook off thoughts of what Kenya was talking about to her. "Oh, she just got here."

"What did she whisper to you?" Abe asked.

Lovely frowned and said, "Well...she said something about knowing who killed my parents. I thought that was really weird. I mean, how does she know about that? I've never talked to Kiera about that. Have you told her?"

"No, I didn't," Abe said curtly. He tried to desist from displaying his anger.

"Isn't that weird though? I mean, why would she say that?"

"I don't know. But let's not worry about that right now," he said taking her hand in his. He brought her hand up to his lips to kiss it endearingly. "We just buried my niece and nephew's mama today. Let's focus on that because with Eli as their only parent now, those kids are gonna need all of the support they can get."

Lovely laughed. "You've got that right. Poor Eli. But he's doing okay."

"He is for today. Let's see how he is by next week. I bet he'll be putting Bria and Bryce out."

"You know what? I'm sure you're right."

———

Sarah followed Robin as she left the repass early. She knew exactly where Robin was off to. Being with *him* at the condo would be comforting.

Sarah has been keeping up with these two lovebirds for the past couple of days but hadn't said much. She was letting Esau hang himself. And as far as Robin she was gathering enough evidence to expose Robin for who she really was. The nerve of her. Then she wanted to seem as if she was interested in Eli. No, Eli deserved so much better. Robin was screwing Esau for Christ's sake! The only reason Sarah hadn't bothered Eli with what she had discovered was because he was already dealing with one major life event. Sarah didn't want to add more to his load. But when the time was right, she would be exposing both Esau and Robin. Sarah just had to play her cards right and carefully.

Sarah had enough of Esau's cheating ways. She had plans long ago of ridding herself of his crazy ass. She always knew he had a thing for younger women; but hell, she's always had a thing for older men. Sarah's thoughts went to Kiera. *Poor child*. Kiera was just one of many young females Esau had preyed upon. Now he had Robin.

Right now, Sarah felt a need to confront both of them. She wanted Esau to know that she knew about his infidelities. He had sworn he wasn't involved with that girl like that. Furthermore, she wanted to remind him that when she divorced his ass that he wasn't getting shit!

Sarah got to the condo and let herself in with the key that she had conveniently had copied. Immediately she could sense something wasn't right. She could hear voices. A male and a female's voice floated in the living room from the back. Sarah slowly made her way towards the back. She couldn't wait to see their faces when they saw that she was there.

"So, what are the plans for Lovely?" Robin asked. This made Sarah come to a stop. She remained still and listened.

"My nephew is handling that," replied Esau.

"What exactly?" Robin asked.

"You sure do ask a lot of questions lady." This voice threw Sarah off. It wasn't Esau that said those words. It was another man that sounded oddly familiar.

"I just wanna be kept informed, so I know what role to play," Robin explained.

"The kidnapping will go as planned."

Who was that? Sarah thought.

Esau said, "And you, baby, will be there to make sure it goes as planned."

"That's right. Lovely trusts you."

Was that who she thought it was?

Robin asked, "So how much will this ransom be for?"

"Twenty million."

"Why so much?" Robin wanted to know.

"That ain't shit compared to what Lovely has."

Robin said, "Why are you doing this? What's in this for you?"

"What's in this for me? Well, let's see...Eliminate Abe and finish off Lovely."

"Wait. So, this isn't just about a kidnapping?" Robin asked for clarification.

"I can't have Lovely meddling and wanting to know information. It'll get back to Lu."

"So, you plan to get rid of them anyway?" Robin queried.

"After you get the money," he said with a menacing tone.

Esau asked, "Will that be a problem for you, Robin?"

"Oh no. I really don't care what you do with them. I just want to know that we will get away with this."

"Don't worry baby. Just continue to do as I tell you," Esau said.

Robin laughed. "You don't have to worry about that. I'm not trying to end up like Kiera."

Sarah couldn't believe what she was hearing. She wondered how Abe would feel about the devious people in his circle. And then Esau and Robin made her literally sick to her stomach. They were a bunch of lying bastards!

Sarah thought maybe it was best if she left without being seen. They wouldn't have to know she had been there. She backed up as quiet as she could.

As she backed up, she bumped into something. A body. Somebody was standing behind her. She turned around with widened eyes. She gasped, "Lo!"

To be continued...........

About the Author

Ada Henderson brings her imagination to life as she writes amazing urban romance fiction under the pseudonym Ivy Symone. Writing has always been a passion of hers even before she realized that's exactly what it was: passion!

The urge to put daydreams to paper began for her at the tender age of ten. The impulse to write was sporadic over the years; but as an adult she picked writing back up, and it served as a therapeutic outlet for her. It wasn't until late 2013 that her mother encouraged her to get published.

Ivy's first debut novel was Why Should I Love You. After that, came Why Should I Love You 2 & 3, Secrets Between Her Thighs 1 & 2, Never Trust A Broken Heart, Crush 1, 2, & 3, Hate To Love You, Stay, If You're Willing, Bad Habitzz, and The Bed We Made. Ivy humbly received two AAMBC awards: 2015 Ebook of the Year and 2015 Urban Book of the Year for her phenomenal Crush series.

She currently resides in Nashville, TN with two of four children in her home. When Ivy is not reading or writing, she's enjoying cooking, watching horror movies all day long, and spending quality time with her friends and family.

CPSIA information can be obtained
at www.ICGtesting.com
Printed in the USA
LVHW04s1543240918
591190LV00011B/1030/P